An Informal Affair
by Heather Gray

I0626328

an Informal Romance novella

<u>Informal Romance Books</u>
An Informal Christmas
An Informal Arrangement
An Informal Introduction
An Informal Date
An Informal Affair
An Informal Reception (coming fall 2018)

Published in the United States of America by Heather Gray
www.heathergraywriting.com

in celebration of my Savior
in memory of my daughter
with pride in my son
with gratitude for my husband

I will rejoice and be glad in your steadfast love,
Because you have seen my affliction;
You have known the distress of my soul,
Psalm 31:7

One

Lia Promise stared at the man across the table from her. This couldn't be happening.

He reached for his fork, pried one of the tines wide, and used it to scratch the inside of his ear.

When had her life turned into this?

Oh yeah, that was right. Maverick was to blame. His ridiculous dare had landed her in this mess.

Even with that dare, she didn't need to subject herself to... whatever passed for normal dinner etiquette in her date's world.

"Look, Albert, it's been swell getting to know you, but I don't think this is working out. At least let me pay for my half of the meal."

Albert eyed her, his brows drawn together. "You sent me the invite. Doesn't that mean you're supposed to pay for the whole meal?"

Lia stared at him. Did the man not understand the concept of dating? Sure, she reached out to him initially, but this date had been his idea. His. Not hers.

She forced a smile to her stiff lips, waved to their waiter, and stood. "Dinner's on me, Albert. Enjoy."

As she sidestepped a server on her way to the cash register, Lia pulled out her phone. She shouldn't take so much delight in telling Maverick all about her bad dates, but doing so had somehow become the highlight of her week.

Lia typed out a text as she waited for the waiter to run her debit card. *Got another whopper for Sunday lunch. You won't believe this one.*

She and Maverick had both been bemoaning the shrinking size of the singles' group at church. Its members had started pairing off at an alarming rate until they couldn't even scrounge up enough people for bowling anymore. So, like sensible God-fearing friends, they'd dared each other to sign up for an online dating service. Because that was what people did in the twenty-first century when they wanted to broaden their social horizons — took to the internet.

Only, Lia hadn't envisioned the plan going quite so horribly wrong.

First there'd been the guy with such a fear of bugs that he'd freaked out and taken off running after a fly dive-bombed his hair outside their restaurant.

Then the one who had brought his mother on their date because, at the age of twenty-seven, he didn't possess a driver's license and refused to use public transit.

Next came the one who described himself as an outdoorsman. How was she supposed to know *outdoorsy* was online dating code for *homeless*? Not every woman could say she'd ended a date by dropping the man in question off at a homeless shelter.

Lia had learned some important lessons during the first month. She now required a minimum of three weeks of online contact before she agreed to meet anybody in person. People's inner weirdness should reveal itself within that time.

Ha.

The joke was on her. Who scratched their ear with a dinner fork? In public? That had to be illegal in at least ten countries. If not, it should be.

The shining light at the end of her bad-date tunnel was the fact that Maverick's luck had been just as atrocious as hers. He was sure to have another horror story from this week's round of disasters…er…dating.

That was how you knew you were friends with someone – when that person's misfortune cheered you up, and you didn't need to feel guilty about it.

Maverick, in khakis and a midnight blue polo, slid into the booth opposite Lia. "Sorry I'm late. One of the ushers thought he saw a mouse, and everybody went crazy. Took a while to calm the masses."

Lia chuckled. "I thought the usher's job was to seat people at the beginning of service. What role do they play when service is over?"

Maverick tapped his fingers on the table. "None, normally, and I don't think today's theatrics did anything to change that."

"I don't like suspense in my movies, books, or lunch conversation. Spill it. What did the usher do?"

"There's a reason you and I don't ever go to the movies together. You realize that, don't you?"

She gave him her best do-as-you're-told stare.

Maverick shook his head, and the diner's fluorescent lights picked up the sable threads that ran through his normally coffee-colored hair. "The usher thought he saw a mouse, and being the good brother-in-Christ he is, he wanted to take care of the problem rather than make more work for someone else."

Lia squinted at him. "How does that lead to a crazy horde of churchgoers?"

He sighed. "It wasn't a mouse. It was one of those curved weird things women use to keep their buns in place. You know, the kind you put the big stick through to hold it on the head? Only, this one was velvet or something."

"And…?"

"The usher thought it was fur. Hence the mouse scare."

Lia set her glass of water down. "It wasn't still… in a woman's hair? Was it?"

Maverick rubbed a hand down his face. "Mrs. Peabody. The usher tried to swat it out of her hair, and her husband took exception to that. He tried to go all Bruce Lee on him. It would have worked, too, if Mr. Peabody wasn't eighty-two years old. Sadly, his Kung Fu days are long behind him. By then, another usher jumped in to restrain Mr. Peabody. So Mrs. Peabody hit him upside the head with her purse."

Lia tried to picture the dignified Mrs. Peabody beating on some poor usher with her purse. "How on earth did you break it up?"

Another sigh.

"One of the women had a whistle. You know, the kind you use for scaring away would-be attackers? So she blew it." He winced. "Boy, was that thing loud. It's a miracle she didn't blow out anybody's ear drums, or the foyer's front windows."

Lia contained her laughter, but barely, and only because they were in public. "So how did you end up involved?"

"I had sound duty today."

"I forgot. Your job is to make sure the mics work without a feedback screech." Why waste time on subtle digs when you knew how to push a friend's buttons?

"Yeah, well, that one wasn't my fault. Somebody messed with my settings." He shuddered. "Anyway, I needed to shut all the equipment down, so I was late leaving the sanctuary. Two minutes

13

sooner, and I'd've been out of there and reading about this on social media rather than replaying the video in my head."

"I guess it's your good luck you were doing sound today, because that video sounds like it's one worth replaying a time or two."

Maverick rolled his eyes.

Their waitress arrived and gave him a pointed look. He obliged with his order. "Double bacon cheeseburger, extra bacon on the side, please."

The waitress turned her attention to Lia, who worked to keep her voice even as she ordered. Nothing was wrong with her order, but compared to Maverick's… "Garden salad, dressing on the side."

As soon as the waitress left, Maverick balled up a napkin and threw it at her. "Come on. You're still upset about that?"

Two weeks ago, she'd met one of her online matches for a first date. Upon seeing her, he'd looked her up and down then smirked. "Your profile didn't say plus-size." That one still smarted. She'd already been struggling with her body image as bad date after bad date had piled up, but that one… She didn't like remembering that date.

Lia did her best to force a casual shrug, not that anything ever really looked casual when forced. "Doesn't hurt to be healthy."

"You're one of the healthiest people I know. Your job is physically active, you work hard, and you take the stairs when most of us slobs are happy to ride in the elevator."

"I can afford to lose a few pounds."

"Whatever." The word came out on a breath as Maverick reached for another napkin. "But don't blame me if some of my bacon accidentally falls into your dressingless salad."

"I got my dressing on the side."

"Which is girl talk for 'I look fat so I'm not eating the dressing but I-don't want anyone to know I'm self-conscious about my weight.'"

He had her pegged. There wasn't much she could say to that. Which made it a perfect time to change the subject. "How'd your date go? Or did you have two this week?"

Maverick fell against the seatback and gripped the edge of the table as though holding on for dear life. "Two. Don't ever let me do that again."

"What was wrong this time? I'm beginning to wonder if you're too picky." Talk about the pot and the kettle...

"No way. Friday night's date was supposed to be five-foot-seven with red hair and green eyes."

"And?"

"Five-foot-two with black hair and glasses so thick I couldn't tell her eye color."

"Being short doesn't automatically make her a bad person."

"No, no. I can forgive short and even accept it was an accident and not outright dishonesty that painted her about five inches taller. Then I asked about her work in avionics. Turns out she works at a hobby shop."

"A hobby shop?"

"Yeah. She sells model airplanes. Which translated to a career in avionics on her dating profile and falls about three steps beyond where I draw the honesty line."

"Ouch. What about Saturday's date?"

He tugged at the edges of his shaggy hair. "She was nice, she really was."

"But?"

"She's deathly allergic to shellfish."

"What happened? You didn't order for her, did you?"

He held up his hands. "No, no. I learned my lesson after the last time. She ordered her own meal. Her glasses — apparently also quite thick — were at home because she wanted to impress her date. I could have told her the ravioli she was ordering had crab in it, but she didn't ask."

"Oh no. Is she okay?"

"An epi pen and a trip to the ER later, yes, she's recovering, but they admitted her to the hospital overnight for observation."

"I think we need to try a new dating site."

"I'm about ready to give up on this whole online dating thing altogether. It's turned out to be more adventure than is strictly good for my sanity. We've both given it a fair shake, but it's just not working. I say we call it quits."

"A friend from work recommended one. It's a Christian site. Maybe you won't run into the same trouble, you know, with people lying about their height and careers and stuff."

He shook his head while saying it, but he still asked, "What's the name?"

"Holy Hearts Matchmaking." She winced. "It sounds hokey, but my friend says they're the best."

"You gonna give them a try?"

Lia rolled a shoulder. "What do I have to lose? Last night's date picked up his dinner fork — the one he'd eaten with — and used it to more or less clean the wax out of his ear."

Maverick choked on his water.

"Then when I said I didn't think we were a match, he stuck me with the entire bill."

"I don't know, Lia. Maybe this online dating stuff isn't for us. Do you think we're being impatient with God's plan? Surely He has someone picked out for both of us, don't you think? Isn't it like testing him or something if we keep pursuing this?"

She leaned back and crossed her arms as the waitress set the dry garden salad in front of her. "The way I see it, we're meeting new people, and that can't be all bad. If one of these people happens to be the person God has for either of us, then all the better. That doesn't mean I'm giving up on looking for someone in the real world, too. But let's face it. This close to DC? Everybody's rushing around. Nobody takes time to get to know each other. It makes meeting people the old-fashioned way almost impossible. "

He sighed. "I'm not sure if it's where we live or a symptom of the era, but I hear you. So what do you think will be different about this Holy Heart place?"

"Holy Hearts. And for starters, there's an extensive statement-of-faith type questionnaire so you can get matched up with someone who believes the same things as you. You know, the big stuff like salvation, but also the little stuff like whether or not women should wear pants to church." She picked up her fork and started waving it around as she talked. "On top of that, you're required to provide evidence that you're a member in good standing of your church."

Maverick tucked a napkin into his lap. "Like a letter from the pastor? I'm not sure I want to go there."

"Me either. They'll take a photocopy of your giving record. You don't have to show the amounts or anything – just the top with the church's name, your name and address, and something that identifies it as having been sent within the last six months. Or a copy of a church directory, but it has to include a picture or address and be dated within a year.

"You think this'll make for better dating experiences?"

Lia put her fork back down. "I hope so. I'm starting to lose faith in the whole system. Now hurry up and say the blessing."

Maverick bowed his head, and Lia followed suit. Silence fell over the table and lasted long enough for Lia to give his shin a light kick. "Today, please."

"Lord, we ask You to watch over Mr. and Mrs. Peabody and the girl from last night with the shellfish allergy. Show us what to do with this whole dating thing. We're both old enough to start thinking about settling down with that permanent someone you have for us, but finding that person is proving more difficult than either of us expected. Amen."

Lia echoed her own, "Amen," before opening her eyes. "Hey…"

Maverick winked at her. "I told you. Bacon. Now eat up. It wouldn't kill you to put some salad dressing on it, either."

Two

What was he going to do with Lia?

Maverick was scratching the surface of thirty and hadn't dated anyone seriously since college. He wasn't itching to settle down, though, so what was the big deal? The online dating had started out as a lark. Neither he nor Lia cared enough to take it to heart. Or so he'd thought.

Thinking always did get him into trouble, though. Which was why responsibility for the entire dating fiasco belonged to him. When the umpteenth couple in their singles' group paired off, Lia had suggested online dating. Maverick, fool extraordinaire, had opened his big mouth and dared her.

Did he dare her to try online dating, though? No. Easy dares belonged on the playground, and they were both too old for that. So he'd gone all in, said they should give it a shot, then dared her to see who could land the worse date.

What kind of a numbskull created a contest where, to win, he must become a bona fide loser? Only someone who didn't plan to take it seriously. So here they were… both with crummy dating records. But at least they got together for lunch on Sundays.

Rehashing the gory details of his dates with Lia had turned out to be fun.

The whole not-taking-it-seriously thing had worked fine, too. Up until Sven. Sven was pure scum as far as Maverick was concerned. He'd taken her skiing... before hooking up with some other woman on the slopes. Lia ended up stranded, and since her family didn't know about the online dating, Maverick had been the lucky one to get the call.

He would have gladly left the world of online dating behind at that point. Larks were only meant to last so long, and they weren't supposed to be quite so painful. After arriving at the lodge bearing witness to the stricken look on her face, though, how could he back out? Her stubborn streak wouldn't let her quit, and his stubborn streak wouldn't let her go through it alone. And so he found himself stuck on the online dating merry-go-round with no exit in sight.

Maybe the Christian service would offer a healthier pool of people to choose from. Hopefully. He didn't want to see Lia tearstained and disappointed again.

Maverick pulled into his driveway and cut the engine before tugging his phone from its holster and punching out a text.

Alright, you win. I'll check out Holy Heart, but I'd better not be alone in this.

His phone buzzed seconds later, and the infamous one-eyed picture filled the screen. He'd been trying to take Lia's picture for his contacts list, but the wind had kicked up at just the right time. Whenever she called now, one hazel eye peeked out from behind a veil of red hair. *Hearts. Holy Hearts. As in it-takes-2. Want help setting up your profile?*

I'm a big boy. I think I can swing it on my own this time.

We'll see about that… I'll set mine up, too. Who knows — maybe we can talk about something pleasant next Sunday!

He let himself in the front door, booted up his laptop, and sat down on the couch. "Alright, Holy Hearts. Don't fail me now. Or, at least don't fail me as much as the last place."

Gender: Male
Age: 25-35
State: Virginia
Marital Status: Never Been Married
Do you smoke? No
Height? 5'10"
Level of Education: Bachelor's Degree
How often do you attend church? Every week
Do you want children? Haven't thought about

it

Are you willing to date someone who already has children? Haven't thought about it
Do you like to try new things? Sometimes
Are you an optimist or a pessimist? Optimist
I don't mind hard work. Agree

On a scale of 1 to 10, 1 being unimportant and 10 being very important, rate the importance of the following items in your own life.

Having a strong work ethic: 10
Honesty: 10
Willingness to try new things: 8
Respecting authority: 9
Following the rules: 9
Sanctity of marriage: 10
Empathy: 7
Emotional intimacy: 7
A tidy home: 7
Getting to work on time: 10
Politics: 7

The list of questions went on for pages. Ninety minutes later, Maverick's finger hovered over his laptop's track pad as he decided how he should answer the final question.

Interested in: Marriage, Dating with an Eye on Marriage, Dating but Definitely Not Marriage, Friendship, Online Relationship Only, Not Sure

Did he want the same thing now as the last time he filled one of these out? It wouldn't be fair — to him or the women involved — if he wasn't honest on this question.

A minute, a quick prayer, and a shake of the head later, Maverick clicked a couple more buttons and closed his laptop.

This had better be worth it.

Three

Lia clicked the submit button and watched as her profile went live on the Holy Hearts site. Surely her luck would improve. Even though she'd said she was only interested in dating Christian men at the last one, she'd ended up with all sorts of people contacting her.

This one would be better. It had to be. But if not, at least she could share her misery with Maverick. He was good at commiserating.

She shut her computer down and got ready for bed. Morning would come early enough, and she needed to be at work by 5:30.

Lia peeked out from the locker room. The ER was bustling, which meant she would be on her feet all day.

She tucked her phone into her pocket, tightened her pony tail, and made her way out into the fray.

"Promise, stitches in 8A!"

Lia nodded to Dr. Zagel and spun toward cubicle 8A. A quick scan of the chart told her who

25

she would be treating. "Hello Mrs. Baxter. I understand you cut yourself on some broken glass."

The young mother held a toddler in her lap and had one arm wrapped around a baby while her other arm, swathed haphazardly in a kitchen towel, hung at her side. "I dropped a glass. I was doing dishes, and my hands were soapy. I was fine until someone screamed, then I turned away from the sink, and the glass slipped and hit the floor. Brodie started crawling toward it, and I went to block him, and...here I am."

Lia smiled. "Not to worry. We'll fix you up right as rain. Is there anyone to help with the kids while I do the suturing?"

She shook her head. "My husband's at work, and he'll get in trouble if he leaves. I don't have any family in the area."

"Alright, let me see if I can find someone to pop in and give us a hand. I'll be back."

Lia stepped back out into the corridor and pulled out her phone. She texted Blossom, one of the volunteer chaplains. *Have a mom with two babies and she needs stitches. Can you come hold a baby or two so I can do my job?*

Be there in 15.

Lia poked her head back around the curtain. "A chaplain is coming down to help with the kids while I get you stitched up. She'll be here in a few minutes. Will you be okay on your own till then?"

26

Mrs. Baxter peered from one kid to the other before nodding mutely.

Lia couldn't imagine the stress. *Sole responsibility for two little lives, and something goes wrong.* If she ever got married and had kids, she wanted to be near family. Life was easier when you had a support system.

"Promise!"

Lia looked up when her name was yelled.

"Done with the stitches?"

She shook her head. "Baby and toddler with her. Waiting on a chaplain. I can spare fifteen minutes if you need me."

Dr. Zagel pointed at cubicle 7D. "High on something, two broken bones, but we can't get him to stay still long enough for us to set them. Can you help restrain?"

She nodded. "Sure. Who's doing the setting?"

"Me. I'm right behind you."

Lia squeezed into the small space as two other nurses attempted to keep the patient still. Today was on course to be anything but boring.

Dr. Zagel pushed through the curtain. "I'm going to do the right femur first. X-ray shows a clean break, should be a simple set, but we can't give him anything for the pain because we don't know what he's on."

"He's not feeling any pain." One of the nurses waggled her eyebrows. "Let's do this before the drugs wear off."

Dr. Zagel stepped up to the bed, directed Lia to hold the patient's left thigh, then pulled hard on the right leg.

"Aaaaaaaagggggggg!"

Unfortunately, the drugs *were* wearing off.

"Left arm next." Dr. Zagel slipped around the side of the bed and grabbed the arm in question. He ordered one of the other nurses to put her weight on the patient's shoulder. Then he pulled without breaking a sweat.

The patient screamed again, but the doctor just nodded to the nurses. "Promise, go check on the mom with stitches. Peters and Jacobs, do his cast. Come find me when you get the first few layers on so I can take a look."

The three nurses all spoke in chorus. "Yes Doctor." Then they shared a grin. Sometimes the doctors needed to think they were the ones in charge.

Lia was about to step into Mrs. Baxter's room when Blossom called her name. "Lia, there you are. Tell me where you need me."

Lia tipped her head toward the curtain before sliding it open. "Alrighty, Mrs. Baxter. This is Blossom. She's going to give us a hand with your kids so I can get you stitched up." Lia picked the toddler up out of his mom's lap and plopped him onto the chaplain's lap. Then she handed the baby over as well. Blossom settled the baby against her shoulder and reached into a bag at her feet to bring out a board book for the toddler.

No doubt the bag was loaded with child-friendly entertainment. Blossom didn't work with kids, but she knew enough to pop into the Child Life offices and grab one of their go-bags before coming down to the ER.

Lia carefully peeled the blood-soaked towel away from Mrs. Baxter's left hand. "How did you get to the hospital? With your husband at work and no family in the area…?"

The woman paled as Lia revealed the bloody gash. "Drove."

Alarm slammed through Lia's chest. "It must have been a challenge to lift the kids into their car seats."

Mrs. Baxter's eyes widened. "I promise… they were in their seats. I can't afford an ambulance. It was drive myself or wait for my husband to get home tonight. I knew I needed a doctor. It's a bad cut, so I did what I had to do."

Lia rested her hand on Mrs. Baxter's arm. "You were smart to come in for stitches. Sometimes I forget how much fortitude moms have when dealing with difficult circumstances."

She reached for the alcohol. "I'm going to clean the wound, and it's going to hurt like the dickens. Do you want anything for the pain before I start?"

"No ma'am. I need to drive home again afterward. And I don't get to sleep on the job, not with these two rug rats." Mrs. Baxter winked at the toddler.

Lia held the cut hand over a disposable pink plastic bowl and poured alcohol over the wound. Mrs. Baxter's eyes flooded with tears, but she made nary a whimper.

"Thanks for the help, Blossom."

"In case you forgot, I don't do kids."

Lia tried to hide her smile. "I was desperate. Child Life won't come down to the ER unless it's a kid we're stitching up."

Blossom's brow furrowed. "That doesn't sound right."

"Not their choice. It came from higher up. Had someone from Child Life been in the ER, I could've grabbed her, but you know how it is. Chaplains are never busy…"

Blossom snorted. "Like ER nurses. We sit around all day and braid each other's hair."

"Promise!" Dr. Zagel's voice rang out.

"Gotta run. Have a good day." Lia jogged over to the doctor's side. "What do you need?"

"A massage would be nice, but I'll settle for your help with an acute abdominal distress in 5A."

Lia arrived at the cubicle in no time, glanced at the chart, and swept the curtain aside. "Hello Mr. Smith. What seems to be the problem today?"

She reached for his hand to check his pulse while he complained that he'd already told three people about his problem and shouldn't be forced to repeat it. In mid-diatribe, Mr. Smith leaned over the side of the bed and retched. He didn't even pause long enough for Lia to jump out of the way. At least most of it landed on her shoes instead of the floor. Less splatter that way.

Dr. Zagel shook his head before poking it back out the curtain. "Salazar! We have a Code V in 5A."

When he looked back at Lia, she summoned a half-hearted smile. "And people wonder why I don't wear tennis shoes to work. If they can't be hosed off, they don't belong on my feet."

Salazar, one of the techs, bustled in with a mop bucket. "Code V, huh? Took me a minute to figure that one out."

The hospital had a policy against using words like *vomit* and *puke* in the ER. For some people, the word alone induced a hypersensitive gag reflex. Each doctor had their own shorthand, but Dr. Zagel stuck with Codes. V for vomit, Brown for fecal matter. Code Slushy meant an urgent bleeding problem. He'd tried Gusher for a while, but the admin hadn't approved of that, so he'd switched to Slushy.

Dr. Zagel had another quirk, too. He called everyone by their last name, a holdover from his days in the Army Medical Corps, no doubt.

Lia wasn't particularly fond of her last name. On the bright side, her parents hadn't named her Eternal like they'd originally planned. They'd been quite the Christian hippies back in the day, or so the story went. Lia's paternal grandparents had come to her rescue, thank goodness, by offering to buy the young couple a car if they refrained from naming the baby Eternal Promise. In desperate need of a vehicle, they'd caved to the pressure.

Lia still sent a thank-you card to her grandparents every year on her birthday. It was the least she could do.

Salazar finished up the floor and wiped down the side of the bed. "Anything else?" He eyed her shoes with barely concealed horror.

"We're good, and I have a clean pair in my locker, so no worries."

She had two clean pairs in her locker. She'd learned that lesson the hard way. Clean socks, too.

Dr. Zagel stepped back in. "Do you feel any better since you threw up, Mr. Smith?"

"Oh yeah, doc, lots better. Thank you. I think I'd like to go home now."

"Still any nausea?"

"A little, but not like it was. No pain or anything, either."

Dr. Zagel nodded as he typed something into his tablet. "I'm going to palpate your abdomen to see if I can feel anything."

Mr. Smith was still asking what palpate meant when Dr. Zagel snapped his gloves on and started moving his hands over the patient's abdomen, stopping every so often to press down. "Did you come here tonight on your own, or did somebody drive you?"

"Girlfriend's out in the waiting room."

"Good. I'm going to have the nurse give you a shot to help alleviate any further nausea you have. The medicine will make you sleepy, so you can't drive or operate heavy machinery for at least six hours after the shot."

"Sure thing, doc."

"If the pain returns, you may want to come see us again."

"You sure it's not my appendix or anything like that?"

Dr. Zagel gave his I'm-done-talking-to-you smile. "That's what I felt around for. It doesn't appear to be your appendix. But like I said, if the pain returns, come on in."

He pivoted toward Lia. "Eight milligrams ondansetron. I just punched it in."

"Yes, Doctor." It wasn't one of the usuals they kept in the ER, and it would take the pharmacy a little while to deliver it. "Mr. Smith, I need to go collect your medication. Can you stay here for me? I'll be back in about fifteen minutes."

He waved his hand. "I'm not going anywhere."

Lia tried to keep herself to a walk as she headed back to the locker room. Only two patients in, and she needed to change shoes. That did not bode well for the rest of the day.

Four

Maverick settled in to eat his lunch. He offered up a short prayer of thanks for the meal and took a bite of his roast beef sandwich.

Lia burst into the room as he was mid-chew. "I have ten minutes, fifteen tops. I need to scarf, but did you check out your phone yet?"

He pulled out his phone and held it up in question.

She rolled her eyes. "Did you install the Holy Hearts app? It gives you real-time data about who's looking at your profile."

He hadn't even thought to look for an app. He was content to confine Holy Hearts to his laptop. Maverick swallowed. "I'm not sure I want that much drama in my life."

Lia took a bite of her salad. "Yeah, because life in Information Technology is riddled with drama."

"Don't knock it. Without us IT guys to keep this hospital running, you nurse types would be in a world of hurt."

She took another bite of her salad. "Did you notice this service gives you a choice of whether or not you let people see your picture? You can decide to let them get to know you without the picture first if you want. Then you choose when they see what you look like."

"Yep. I decided to keep my handsome mug hidden."

Lia frowned. "What if nobody contacts you then?"

He shrugged. "Then they weren't interested enough in me to begin with."

Another bite. "You're playing hard-to-get, aren't you?"

Maverick chuckled. "Anybody ever tell you not to talk with your mouth full?"

"Ten minutes. Fifteen tops. What part of that didn't you understand?"

She shoved another bite of salad into her mouth as someone pushed the door open. "Lia, you're needed in the pen!"

She gave a quick wave as she took off, still chewing her last bite. For some reason that remained a mystery to him, the ER was referred to as the bullpen, or pen for short. He'd thought of asking if the patients were the bulls or the cowboys, but he'd worked around medical personnel long enough to know a thing or two — like when not to ask something.

Maverick picked up the remains of Lia's lunch. She'd run off without putting it away. He went to click the lid onto her salad bowl when he stopped to take a closer look. Lettuce and celery, no dressing.

As he slid the bowl back into her insulated lunch bag, he couldn't help but take note that the only other thing in there was a fat free, low-calorie plain yogurt.

He shuddered.

Gross.

How did Lia have so much energy when she ate like a rabbit during a famine?

"How was your week?" Lia's cheeks were flushed as she slid into the booth opposite Maverick.

"You're running late today. Please tell me there wasn't another mouse incident." He wouldn't wish that madness on anybody.

"I had children's church, remember? I thought I texted you."

"Yeah, but you're usually here by now."

"There was a new kid, and her dad wanted to ask some questions when he picked her up."

Something in Lia's voice… "Dad, huh? Where was Mom?"

She broke eye contact and unwrapped her silverware. "I didn't ask, but she's obviously not in the picture. No wedding band, and little Lucie didn't mention her mom even once."

"He didn't ask you out, did he?"

"Don't be silly. We barely met."

Maverick's antenna remained on high alert. "What's his name?"

She tucked her napkin away on her lap. "Don't go all weird and protective on me. We were talking. He didn't get down on bended knee or anything."

The subject wasn't over, not by a long shot, but maybe it was time for a tactical retreat. "Did you have a date this week?

She shook her head. "I decided to stick to my three week rule."

"It's a good rule." He hoped she applied the same discriminating judgment to strange men she randomly met at church.

"What about you? Any dates to dish on?"

"No dates yet, but I've started talking to a couple of women."

"Yeah, me too. Only men. Not women."

"I saw Samantha Willard."

Lia's brow crunched. "At church today?"

"Holy Hearts."

Samantha used to be in the singles' group at church. When she stopped coming, they'd all assumed she had a serious boyfriend somewhere.

"Oh, wow. I guess things didn't work out with the mysterious boyfriend." Lia tucked her hair behind her ear. "Either that or she finally accepted that the pool of eligible men at church had shrunk beyond all hope. Short of going around and kissing random frogs, she never would have found anyone to date. So, did you message her?"

He shook his head. "No, that seemed weird. Besides, there was never a spark when we saw each other on a regular basis. I doubt that's changed. And I kind of decided with Holy Hearts not to message the women. I'll respond to the ones who contact me, but I'm taking a break from chasing women down."

"Samantha's nice. Do you get many women contacting you? Sometimes I worry if being the first to make contact means I'm too aggressive."

"No complaint against Samantha, but she's not the one. As for aggression, nah. Not in today's world, anyway."

Laughter sparkled in Lia's hazel eyes. "So you think there's only one? Do you call her your…" She batted her eyes. "…soul mate?"

This time Maverick rolled his eyes. "I don't think we're limited to just one. We mess things up too much for that. If God had only one person for each of us, this world would be a disaster with an even higher divorce rate than it already has. But I do think when you meet someone with whom you can make it work, something inside tells you."

"What does it sound like? How do you know?"

The waitress arrived, and not a moment too soon. The conversation had taken an uncomfortable turn toward girly emotional stuff. "Bacon cheeseburger, extra bacon on the side, and seasoned fries."

Lia eyed him. He had to order the bacon on the side if he wanted to slip it into her salad. On the burger it would be all coated with meat juice and cheese.

"Chicken Caesar Salad, dressing on the side. Separate checks, too, please."

The waitress' eyebrow went up, but she didn't say anything.

Maverick opted not to defend himself with the *we're-just-friends* spiel. Trying to change her mind now would only make it worse.

The waitress left, but not before sending a healthy scowl in Maverick's direction.

"I hope she doesn't spit in my food."

Lia's lips pursed. "People don't actually do that, you know. And it's not like you did anything to upset her, so why would she?"

"She thinks I'm your date and that I'm too cheap to pay for your food."

Lia's eyes grew wide, laughter reflected in the hazel pools. "Oh dear. That's too funny." She fought to get her mirth under control. "Would you like me to explain it to her? I could tell her that you're not a cheap date. You're just a cheap friend…"

"Gee, thanks, but I think I'll pass. You're a peach for offering, though." Maverick reached for his water.

Some guy would to be lucky — no, blessed — to have Lia for a wife someday. No matter how bad — or boring — the week had been, she always found something to laugh about.

Five

A warm cup of lentil soup and a hot shower behind her, Lia sat in bed, her phone in-hand.

She'd started daydreaming about potato chips halfway through her soup, but chips had salt, and salt retained water. Good thing she didn't have any chips in the house, or she'd probably give in to the craving.

Lia forced her attention away from thoughts of food and back to the Holy Hearts app on her phone.

Eighteen new people had viewed her profile that day, but only two messaged her. Bob and Rick. Ever since her last two-hour stint on the phone with tech support — to get something as simple as her DVR working — she harbored an innate dislike of anyone named Bob.

It wasn't, however, fair to judge all Bobs by one, so she read through his profile. He worked in automotives — which could mean used car salesman — and had been divorced twice. Divorce happened. She got that. But… Two seemed like more baggage than she wanted to take on. Not one to give up easily, she kept reading. He'd marked smoking as *occasional*. She wasn't a fan, not at all, but she didn't want to be too critical, either. Under previous convictions, though, when his answer said *would prefer to discuss in person*, she clicked out of his profile.

She didn't mind some baggage, but this guy had more luggage than a Hollywood princess.

Lia moved over to Rick's profile. Late 20s, gainfully employed, not a smoker, never been arrested. He was a veritable knight in shining armor compared to Bob. She tapped the button to open the message he'd sent.

> *Hey. These profiles are pretty impersonal, but yours caught my eye. Maybe we could visit online a bit and get to know each other.*

Okay, so he wasn't the most talkative guy in the world. She could live with that. She talked enough for two people anyway. Time to send him a reply…

> *Hey Rick. You're spot-on about the profiles being impersonal. So…getting to know each other better…what does that look like for you? Do you want me to talk about myself, or do you have questions you want to ask? For now, I'll ask one. Let's start with… Where were you born?*

Rick's profile picture was hidden, and he worked with computers. That didn't tell her much.

A couple seconds after she hit *send*, a new message popped up in her inbox.

> *Huh. We must be online at the same time. I guess that makes sense. We're*

in the same time zone, and almost everyone's work day is over.

> *So, to answer your question, I was born in Virginia, and I've lived here my whole life. What about you? Where are you from? Ever been anywhere exotic? (I went on a mission trip to West Virginia once. That's about the most exotic place I've been.)*

A man with a sense of humor. She could appreciate that. Lia typed out her reply.

> *Born in Maryland, but I've lived in Virginia since the age of two. Or since my sister turned two. I can never remember the story, but one of us was definitely two.*
>
> *As for exotic places, I go into DC every once in a while. It's pretty exotic with people from all over the world. Does that count?*

She hit send and waited. Five minutes passed with no reply, so she decided to go through some other profiles and see if anyone interested her enough for a HeartGram, Holy Hearts' version of email.

A brief search revealed three men who might be interesting. Zeke, a firefighter; Michael, a community support specialist — whatever that meant; and Rod, who worked with computers. Which could mean anything from programming to retail sales. Only one way to find out.

She shot a quick message off to all three.

> *Saw your profile and thought it*
> *might be worth getting to know each other a*
> *little better. Let me know if you agree.*

Ha. Her message was even shorter than Rick's.

When she'd first ventured into the world of online dating, Lia had sent lengthy messages with each introduction. It took a while for her to realize a third of the men were never going to reply. Since she didn't like wasting energy, she'd started to make her introductions shorter but still personal. Eventually, however, she gave up on personal altogether. They would go straight to her profile and decide from there whether or not they wanted to respond, anyway, so why bother? Witty repartee was squandered on an introductory message. She would save her charm and effervescence for any follow-up conversation that might occur.

She clicked back over one more time to see if she'd heard back from Rick.

Nada.

Oh, well. Now she had time to surf social media before going to bed.

Six

"You look like death."

Lia dragged her eyes up to stare at Maverick. "I need more coffee."

He chuckled and moved aside. Never get between a woman and the coffee pot. As far as life mottos went, it was a solid one. It had served him well working in a hospital, too.

Once she took a drink, she nodded to him. "What are you doing here anyway? I thought IT guys usually stayed up on the fifth floor."

"Network's down in the ER. Your workstations and tablets aren't able to access patient records from the main database. You can't tell if someone's a return client, and even if they tell you this is their fiftieth visit, you won't be able to access their file."

"Great."

Keeping patient records connected was vital. To effectively treat a patient, the staff needed to know if the patient suffered from a drug allergy or pre-existing condition. Not to mention the drug-seekers. Maverick hadn't realized what a problem drug-seekers were until Lia educated him about it one day. Without access to patient records, the nurses couldn't tell which patients were flagged.

Yep. The network was a priority, which was why his pager had sounded at four o'clock that morning. He'd dragged himself into work before the reasonable people of the world were stirring from their beds.

Maverick tossed his paper cup into the garbage can and tweaked the end of Lia's nose. "Back to the salt mine for me."

"Got it fixed yet, Hoyt?"

Maverick glanced up to discover his supervisor hovering over his left shoulder. "Almost. Not sure how it happened, but it looks like the router port that serves the ER stopped working."

"Good, good."

"I'll be filing a security report directly with corporate when I'm done."

Maverick's boss turned a sickly shade of green. "Is that necessary?"

"Either this happened accidentally, or it was intentional. No matter how you look at it, a part of our system that's supposed to be locked down tighter than Fort Knox has been breached. It needs to be reported, and the security keys need to be changed again."

This was the third such incident in the past four months, making it far too frequent for Maverick's peace of mind. He didn't have the proof to back it up, but it felt like the hospital's network was under attack. To make matters worse, he'd handed the last two security reports over to Mr. Planter for filing, but the man had scuttled them both. Neither had been sent up the chain of command.

His boss frowned. "Fine, if you must. Do you suppose they'll want us to bring in that cybersecurity team they've been talking about?"

Maverick didn't bother answering. He certainly hoped someone was brought in, though. The hospital, part of a bigger conglomeration, had access to an entire team of cybersecurity specialists. The extra help would be useful. He did, however, know better than to tell his boss so. The man was a nervous sort who seemed to constantly be in fear of losing his job. Maverick wasn't in the mood to smooth things over with the man. Best not to ruffle his feathers in the first place.

"How's that… What are you eating?"

Maverick looked sidelong at Lia, who had come into the break room not two minutes before. "A Monte Cristo."

"Where do you come up with all these fancy sandwiches?" She took out her plastic container of salad and bowed her head.

He waited till she was done before answering. "A coffee joint in my neighborhood. The guy's branching out into food and likes to try the new menu items on me."

"So, what, you stop in for your morning coffee and sometimes he gives you food, too? What happens if there's no sandwich?"

"If he doesn't offer me something new to test out, I buy a sandwich off the menu."

Lia took a bite of her salad. "Must be terrific to be able to buy lunch whenever you want. Are you better off than I realized? Maybe I should start making you pay for our Sunday lunches."

Maverick wiped his mouth and hands with his napkin before reaching for his bottle of water. "Not well-off. Better connected. And I'm not saving every spare penny to get a new car."

She frowned at him. "You make it sound like that's a bad thing. What's gonna happen when your car bites the dust?"

"It's not bad. In fact, I admire it. I can't help but wonder sometimes, though, if you're making yourself miserable with saving so much. I still tuck money aside each month for my car. Whatever doesn't go toward repairs will be there someday when I need a new one. The difference between us is that I choose not to save until I end up too broke for coffee and sandwiches."

"Makes sense. I could do that, too, if I weren't so sure my car is planning to die any day now."

A quick glance at his phone told Maverick his lunch break was over. "Any luck with the new dating profile?"

"A few nibbles, one of them seems pleasant enough. We'll see if it goes anywhere." She gave a half-hearted shrug.

"Gotta run. I'll catch you later."

He dropped his trash in the bin and headed back up to the fifth floor. The break room on his floor was a replica of the one by the ER, but the conversation up there fell short of interesting.

Lia slid into the booth across from Maverick, and her sigh spoke volumes. "How do you *always* beat me here?"

She'd gotten there first plenty of times, but he kept that thought to himself.

"You could just ride with me, you know. Then I could swing you back by church to pick up your clunker."

Her red hair billowed around her face as she shook her head. "Uh-uh. No way. No how."

"Remind me again why you can't bear to be seen in the same vehicle with me?" Maverick lifted an eyebrow as he waited for her answer.

Lia's eye roll said it all. "One car ride together, and people will think we're dating."

"Ah, now I remember." He reached across and gave her hand a playful pat. "That's why we drive thirty minutes away from church to share a meal, so nobody thinks we're interested in each other."

"Exactly." With a firm nod, Lia picked up her menu.

Maverick didn't have the heart to tell her the reason none of the men at church asked her out was because they already thought she was spoken for… by him. How had he managed to land himself in this pickle? Oh yeah, that was right. By speaking up when he should have kept quiet.

Speaking of which… "Did that single dad single you out again?"

Lia rolled her eyes. "You need to go back to pun school."

Maverick chuckled. "Hey, that wasn't even a pun. It was word play. So, did you talk to him?"

She snagged his glass of water and took a drink from the rim, ignoring his straw. "His name's Mark. Seems like a nice guy. His daughter's a cutie, too."

Why was his gut all twisted up? He wanted Lia to find a man who deserved her. Was God trying to tell him something about this guy? "Just remember the three-week rule."

"Yes, Mother."

Their waitress approached, and Lia gave her a bright smile. "Caesar salad, dressing on the side please. Separate checks."

"You want chicken on that Caesar?"

Lia bit her bottom lip, so Maverick cut her off before she could say no. "She wants chicken on it. Give me a double bacon cheeseburger with seasoned fries and an extra side of bacon."

The waitress gave a long-suffering sigh before walking off.

"You shouldn't order for a woman. It's presumptuous." Lia's glare could have singed the eyebrows off a hairless Chihuahua.

He lifted his hands. "I know, I know. You and at least two of my dates have told me before. But…" Maverick swallowed some air. "You need to eat something besides rabbit food."

"I'm not too skinny." She crossed her arms and stared.

Maverick stretched his arms out along the seatback. What was Lia's problem? "I never said you were too skinny. I think you look great. You've been losing weight, though, and I'm not sure it's in a healthy way. A little protein won't hurt you. Unless you've developed an allergy. Will the chicken make you break out in hives?"

"You always order extra bacon and stick it in my salad. You're trying to fatten me up, aren't you? What's your diabolical plan?"

Maverick chuckled. "Rest assured, I'm not a witch, and this restaurant isn't made of gingerbread. I have no plans to fatten you up or to toss you into the oven."

Color climbed Lia's cheeks. "Sorry."

Biting at people wasn't Lia's usual way, and Maverick had no intention of letting it drop. That guy who'd made the plus-size remark needed to be throttled. "Want to tell me what's going on?"

Her stare slid sideways to the salt and pepper shakers, but her hand snaked past them to the container of colored sweetener packets. She dumped them out on the table and started sorting them by color. Then flipped them so they all faced the same direction.

Maverick stretched a hand across the table and stopped her. "What happened?"

She lifted her gaze, and the sight of tears pooling in her hazel eyes pushed him back into his seat.

Lia pulled her hand out from under his and reached for a napkin. "It's nothing. I just overreacted to something.

Maverick had only ever seen Lia get this upset about one thing, and Mr. Plus-Size was too far in the past to be responsible. "Did you go on a date Friday night?"

She remained silent and continued to focus on the sweetener packets.

"Do I get a name?"

"Armand."

"Should I polish my brass knuckles? Because I'm happy to go have a chat with Armand."

The corner of her mouth lifted. "Armand's not the problem. He…" Lia tucked the sweeteners back into their container and brushed the hair out of her face. "He's from the old dating service. He contacted me before I canceled my profile over there."

Pushing Lia to answer a question never got him anywhere. He'd have to let her take the scenic route. "So tell me about Armand, then."

The clouds began to clear in Lia's eyes as laughter flashed in their place. "His profile said he enjoyed sports. I thought that meant he was athletic."

"Let me guess…"

The waitress set their meals in front of them as Lia answered his unspoken inquiry. "He only enjoys watching sports. On television, not even in person."

"Ahh…"

"And that television?" The corner of her mouth quirked up.

"In the basement of his parents' house?"

"Worse. But let's pray first."

Maverick bowed his head and asked a blessing over their meal. As soon as they uttered their *amens*, Lia reached for her fork, and he took the opportunity to slide his extra bacon into her salad bowl.

She frowned at him, and the storm clouds came rolling back into her eyes. He hoped she reached the point of the story before too much longer. He'd like to avoid the landmines only women seemed to see. "So what's worse than his parents' basement?"

Lia nudged the bacon aside with her fork before picking up a mouthful of lettuce sans salad dressing.

Seven

Lia chewed the dry and tasteless salad. It begged for dressing, but her stubbornness refused to allow it. She usually asked for the dressing on the side so she could give her salad a light drizzle instead of the ginormous dousing most restaurants delivered. Maverick had gotten all territorial about her eating habits, though, and ordered for her. Now she couldn't put any dressing on her greens. It was the principal of the matter.

"So?" Maverick's eyebrow lifted as she continued to chew on what he rightly referred to as rabbit food. "What's worse than his parents' basement?"

Lia forced her bite of salad down. Who needed dressing anyway? Or the calories it brought.

Maverick was right. She'd been losing weight. Even her drawstring scrubs were getting loose on her. She had weight to spare, though. He didn't need to make such a big deal out of it.

She reached for her water but set it back down before she took a drink. Friday night's date had been horrible, her worst in a long time. Maybe talking it over with Maverick would help her find the humor in it.

She could use some humor.

All she'd managed to find so far were the ugly feelings stirred up inside her, but telling Maverick about her dates — even the colossal failures — always managed to make her laugh.

He dragged a fry through the ketchup dripping down from his burger and onto the plate and stuffed it in his mouth as he stared at her.

She shook her head and sighed. "His parents kicked him out of their basement."

To give him credit, the corner of Maverick's mouth barely lifted. "So where does he live then?"

"With his grandparents."

The other corner of his mouth lifted. "In their basement?"

He was having entirely too much fun with this.

"You're killing me here. If not his grandparents' basement, then where?"

"They're at an assisted living facility."

"And…?"

A small laugh escaped. "Overnight guests aren't allowed."

His cobalt eyes danced with mirth before his smile spread wide. "So then…?"

"He's a stowaway."

It shouldn't be possible for eyebrows to go that far north. "A stowaway?"

She battled her laughter valiantly. Tears pooled in her eyes as she fought to get the words out before she gave in to the hilarity, but they were the good kind of tears. "He hides in their room and sleeps in their closet at night so nobody can find him."

His eyes grew wide. "Please tell me you're joking."

Lia shook her head.

Maverick's bark of laughter filled the diner. "What does this catch do for a living?"

"I thought his profile said he was a network engineer."

"But…?"

"I misread it." Another giggle passed Lia's lips. Grown, dignified women didn't giggle. She should know better. "Apparently he's a Network Elf named Ne'er."

Maverick threw his head back and laughed again. "He listed his level on Network Knights." He ground the heels of his hands against his eyes. "As his occupation." The sound of his laughter abated, but his shoulders continued to shake.

"He's trying to make his way up to being an…" Attempting to hold in her laughter was like asking a punctured balloon to hold its helium. "He's trying to get to the next level so he can be a Network Orc."

Yep. Her dating life had hit an all-time low. She'd gone out with an elf who lived in his grandparents' closet…and saw nothing wrong with that arrangement. Lia shuddered.

Why couldn't she find a man like Maverick? One who worked a real job, lived in a real home, had real friends, and went to a real church?

Holy Hearts had better deliver. The elf had marked *Christian* on his profile, but only because he ultimately wanted to become a Network Druid which somehow meant he had spiritual aspirations. He'd gone on to explain that all religions were the same, so he'd check-marked every single box under the *Religion and Spirituality* section of his user profile.

Did people actually think that way? Surely not. In her line of work, she met tons of people who didn't share her faith. They still recognized that differences existed among the different faiths, though. To think they were all the same seemed so…strange.

Lia sat back in the booth, studied her dry-as-a-bone-left-in-the-Sahara-desert-for-three-months salad, and picked up her fork. She could choke it down. She needed to eat, after all, and since she refused the use of dressing, her choices were limited.

Before she could get the offensively tasteless vegetables into her mouth, Maverick brushed his fingers against her forearm. "So your Network Elf is the reason you got mad at me about the bacon?"

Oh. Why'd he have to go and remember *that* part of their conversation? "Not exactly."

"Seriously. I'm happy to dust off my brass knuckles if you need me to."

Ha. Maverick was as likely to own brass knuckles as the Network Elf. At least if Maverick owned them, they'd be real and not in some virtual video game treasure chest.

Lia set the untouched forkful of salad back in her bowl. "He said something that upset me. No need to go all Neanderthal on me."

"Let's see… You reacted when I mentioned your weight. So what'd the guy say?"

Was she really as transparent as all that?

"I'm just guessing here, but I'd say your interested-in-sports date who watches all his sports on TV is probably not the buffest dude around…?"

"He gives my Uncle Marty a run for his money." Uncle Marty referred to his midsection as a root beer belly. His wife called it a cupcake graveyard.

Maverick bit his bottom lip, his stare intense.

"He was disappointed in my appearance, that's all. He expected something different."

His eyes drilled straight into her. "He didn't dare call you fat."

Lia shook her head. "Said I was too skinny and needed more meat on my bones if I wanted to attract a real man."

Maverick's hands bunched into fists where they rested on either side of his plate. "I'm sorry, Lia. For men everywhere, and for my thoughtless comment earlier, I'm sorry."

She shrugged.

"The guy's a jerk, and you're better off without him."

Lia picked up her fork again, then set it down and stared at the tureen of salad dressing. Should she? "Why do you always try to sneak bacon onto my plate?"

Maverick ran a hand through hair the color of dark chocolate before sitting back and dropping both hands into his lap. "I don't want to see you starving yourself because of this online dating. It's your life, and I don't have the right to tell you how to eat. I... I worry about you, though. You've had some loser dates, and you used to always say bacon is your comfort food." Color climbed Maverick's neck. "I don't know. I thought I was helping. Ever since that jerk made the plus-size remark..." He broke eye contact. "I just want to help."

Lia glanced at her salad dressing one more time before shaking her head and reaching for the tureen. "Don't think this means I'm going to start letting you have your way."

Maverick nodded, a twinkle in his eyes, as she drizzled dressing. "Wouldn't dream of it."

Two bites later, Lia asked the all-important question. "What about you? Any dates this week?"

He grinned. "I attended a meeting with one of the women I met."

What kind of date took place at a meeting? "Um…is she an addict?"

Maverick shook his head as he reached for his burger again. "She does a lot of mission work. We went to an informational get-together for an upcoming mission trip to Indonesia. I expressed an interest, and she asked if I'd like to tag along."

"How do you top that? Do you have to actually sign up for the mission trip to get a second date?"

"As if a woman would ever make it that simple." Maverick polished off the last of his burger. "I'm thinking about going on a mission trip at some point, but we already decided we're better off as friends."

"No spark?"

He shrugged. "It doesn't matter. She wants to spend her life in overseas missions, and I don't feel God calling me to that. I'd like to go on an overseas mission trip, but I don't think that's the life God has for me."

"Gonna give me a name, or do I have to pry it out of you?"

Color climbed Maverick's neck. "Alexa."

Lia tapped his shin with her foot under the table. "You know I'm teasing, right?"

"Tease all you want, but I'm being a gentleman."

Maverick's idea of being a gentleman was to protect the names of women he'd met online. He only supplied a name once they'd gone out on a real, live date. Or apparently a mission trip informational meeting.

She'd never tell him so to his face, but most women found *gentlemanly* to be a synonym for *sexy*.

Lia took a healthy bite of bacon. "Only one date this week?"

"Hey, you're the one who said we should get to know people before we meet them in-person. Remember? You wanted to get off on the right foot at Holy Hearts and not jump straight into the deep end. I distinctly remember a lecture to that effect."

"I don't lecture."

"Ha! Tell that to my baby sister."

"I was her babysitter! What did you expect? That I would let her lasso passing cars while wearing roller skates? And don't get me started about the time she thought she'd jump out of her window during a lightning storm. If ever a girl needed a lecture, she did."

Maverick chuckled. "Yeah, well, that wild child is coming home on leave in a couple of days, and Mom wants you to come over for a barbecue after church next Sunday. Think you can manage?"

"Wouldn't miss it."

"Good. Because she says she has a surprise for you."

"Your mom or Watts?"

"Watts, of course. Why do you think I'm warning you?"

Lia swallowed her fear. The last time Maverick's sister had presented her with a surprise, she'd ended up in the ER, and not as a nurse.

IGHT

Worst idea ever.

Maverick stared at the throbbing vein in his supervisor's neck. Then he closed his eyes and tried counting to ten, hoping he'd open them to find this meeting was a bad dream.

He only made it to three before he peeked.

Nope, not a dream.

His supervisor, Mr. Planter, continued to stare daggers at him, and Butch Hutchinson, the other man in the meeting, seemed delighted by the strife he'd managed to stir up with his appearance.

"I told you I would be filing a report." Maverick wasn't in the wrong, and he knew it. Why was his supervisor being so obstinate about the whole thing? "The system's been hacked. There's no way around it. The cybersecurity team can help us figure out what's going on."

"I would have asked for help if I'd needed it." Mr. Planter drummed his fingers on the conference room table.

"Gentlemen, gentlemen, there's no need to argue. We all want the same thing, don't we?"

Maverick flicked his gaze toward the polished man with shrewd eyes and a big, shiny Rolex. "I don't know. Do we? Because showing up unannounced and demanding a meeting where you drop a bombshell and sit back to see who's going to throw who under the bus doesn't give me the impression that you want the same thing I do."

Mr. Planter sputtered. "What he said!"

Mr. Hutchinson leaned forward and steepled his fingers. "Very well. Why don't we start over?" He ignored Mr. Planter and held out a manicured hand toward Maverick. "My name's Butch. It's a pleasure to meet you."

Mr. Planter's face transformed, becoming an alarming shade of purple, as Maverick reached his hand out and shook Butch Hutchinson's. They might untangle this mess, but the chances of him still having a job when all was said and done were getting slimmer by the minute.

"What brings you to the ER? More network trouble?"

Maverick winced at Lia's innocent question. "Something like that."

"Why the long face?"

He shook his head. "Long story. Are you off soon?"

She nodded. "I finished passdown, so I'm done for the night."

Dark circles under her grey eyes turned her normally pale skin ghostlike. "Do you work tomorrow?"

Lia gave a quick shake of her head. "Day off, thank goodness. It's been a long couple of days."

"Let me take you out to dinner. You can listen to me complain about my job. Then I'll give you a lift back to the hospital so you can pick up your car."

She inspected him for the better part of a minute. "Will nobody else listen to you whine?"

Maverick almost reached out to tug on her ponytail. "Men don't whine. We vent."

One of her eyebrows lifted. "You know the implication there is that women whine."

He took a step back and held his hands in front of him. "Women don't whine either. Ever."

Her eyebrow stayed up.

"Women…uh… Women share their feelings in a, uh, healthy and productive manner."

Seconds ago, Lia had looked ready to fall asleep on her feet. In an instant, though, the fatigue vanished, leaving laughter in its wake. "You men could learn a thing or two from us women." She spun on her heel and headed toward the ER locker room. "Be back in a flash."

Maverick watched her go. The sway of her hips made him think of... Uh-oh. Not going there. He was firmly in the friend zone, and thoughts like that did *not* belong in the friend zone. Thoughts like that were for people in the dating zone.

Had the Network Elf had those kinds of thoughts?

Maverick gritted his teeth. Thoughts like that didn't belong in the dating zone, either, then. They should be reserved for the engaged zone. If some random man Lia went out with entertained thoughts like he'd just had, Maverick would have to deck the guy. No question.

So definitely not okay in the dating zone.

Thoughts like that belonged in the engaged zone, at least. Or the married zone. That was the only safe place for them.

He and Lia were neither of those, so those thoughts positively, absolutely didn't belong in his head.

At all.

"Are you going to stand there all day, or are you going to tell me where we're going?"

Maverick blinked a couple of times before his vision cleared and he saw Lia standing there with her arms crossed. He tried to grin at her, but it felt as stiff as a ceramic drama mask. "Sure, let's go."

Any other time, he would have draped his arm across her shoulders. They were friends. They'd known each other for eons. They were comfortable and familiar. Things between them had always been easy.

Not now though. Suddenly, comfortable and easy were the absolute last words he would use to describe their relationship.

Why'd he have to go and notice her hips? And in scrubs, for pity's sake! Nobody was supposed to look good in scrubs.

"Yoo-hoo." Lia waved her hand in front of his face. "Are you going to open the door for me or not?"

They were at the staff exit, and Maverick had no recollection of the walk there. "Sorry. A lot on my mind." Maverick pulled on the door, but it didn't budge. *Drat.* As if he hadn't gone through this door hundreds of times, he'd forgotten to push.

"Whatever you need to vent about must be important. Are you sure I shouldn't drive?"

Maverick tried to shake the weird not-friend-zone cobwebs from his mind. "Zoned out. Sorry."

He pushed the door open and held it for Lia.

He needed to get the craziness in his head under control before he completely ruined the best friendship he'd ever had. *I could use some help here, God. I don't know what happened back there, but could you wash that image out of my mind? Please?*

It wasn't like it had been a *dirty* image or anything. But it hadn't been a friend-zone image,

71

either. Friends did not notice the sway of their friends' hips. Period.

Maverick stared at his burger. "Um… How was your day?"

Lia reached across the table and nabbed one of his fries. "I'm starving. Don't mind me. I got five minutes for lunch and barely took one bite before getting called back to work."

It was good to see her eating. Maybe she was finally over Plus-Size Jerk and Network Elf Jerk.

He said nothing else, and she stepped in to fill the silence. "Other than that, the usual. I dove out of the way of someone vomiting only to end up with a trainee who had trouble putting in an IV. Blood went everywhere."

He winced. "Any sterilization protocols in place? Or whatever they call it?" He couldn't remember everything about her nursing job, but he knew the nurses ran a risk whenever they came into contact with blood. No one could tell by looking at someone whether or not they had a blood-borne disease.

She frowned. "I'm fine, but the trainee ended up with blood in her mouth, which of course led to more vomiting that I managed to dodge."

Blood in the mouth… Maverick shuddered. Computers were so much safer than people, even if he did have to put up with a supervisor that would rather protect his job than sort out a serious problem. "Is she going to be okay?"

Lia frowned. "They're doing a complete blood workup on the patient to determine if the trainee has anything to worry about. She was sent home for the day, too, but that was mostly because she freaked out. We have so many safety protocols in place as it is that even if she did somehow get infected, there'd be no way for her to pass it on to a patient. But it is what it is. She'd already scheduled some vacation time for a trip with her family. The test results should all be in before she returns, even if it's just for her own mental well-being. Hopefully she's fine because I can tell you, this is one lesson she won't ever forget. No point going through the lesson if you're not going to return to the job."

Maverick was in mid-chew when Lia pointed her fork at him. "We're here so you can vent, and you're quiet as a church mouse."

A picture of Mrs. Peabody swinging her purse at one of the ushers flitted through his mind. He put his burger down and wiped his hands on his napkin. "Remember when the ER got cut off from the main hospital network?"

She nodded.

"It may have been intentional. The router port for the ER failed, but it wasn't a hardware issue. It looks like someone turned it off via software."

Her brow furrowed. "Why would someone do that?"

"No clue, but that's not the problem."

She stabbed a piece of hardboiled egg with her fork. "Seems to me like that's quite a problem."

He took a long draw on his water. "I filed an incident report, and the hospital's cybersecurity team has been called in to investigate the situation."

"We have a cybersecurity team? Then how could something like that happen?"

"The team's not ours. It belongs to Ferito Technology, the corporation that owns the hospital."

"Whoa."

"Yeah." Maverick reached for the salt and added more to his fries. "A cybersecurity team owned by a global technology company. These guys are no lightweights, and the fact that they're here has transformed my supervisor from someone who's perpetually irritable and lazy into someone who's angry and looking for anyone he can find to take the blame."

"And since you filed the incident report…"

"Yep. I'm sure the cybersecurity team will get to the bottom of things, but I'm equally sure that once they move on from here, I'll be out of a job."

"What's your supervisor's name? Planet?"

Maverick shook his head. "Planter. Mr. Planter."

She waved her fork again. "Yeah, yeah, yeah. Planter. Whatever. What makes you so sure Mr. Planter will fire you once the dust settles?"

Maverick exaggerated the wince that came naturally. "I was leaving today when he told me I should spend the evening polishing my résumé."

"Ouch." Lia ate the last bite of her salad and leaned back in the booth. "Can't you just go to HR and explain the situation if he tries to fire you?"

"He'd still be my supervisor. It's a hospital. A nurse who's unhappy with her job can go to work in another department. Switch to cardiology or something. There's only one IT department, though, and that department has all of one supervisor. Unless I want to start taking people's temperature, I can't escape Mr. Planter."

"Hm. Doesn't seem fair."

"Yeah, well, this is the real world, right? I find a way to make it work, or I find another job. Those are my two choices."

"What are you going to do?"

Maverick popped the last fry into his mouth. "I want to stick around long enough to see what the cybersecurity team uncovers."

"You're really interested in that stuff, aren't you?"

"I'm curious."

75

"Maybe you should apply for a job with Ferito Tech. I'm sure they have openings all the time."

He frowned. "I'll wait for the investigation to wrap up. If they find gross negligence on the side of the IT department, then I'm pretty sure any application I submit will be summarily ignored."

Lia stretched her hand out across the table and rested it on his. "God's got this. Whether you stay at the hospital or not, it'll all work out."

His job situation might be okay eventually, sure. His heart was another story altogether. The second she'd touched his hand, his heart had gone into double-time and mocked every friend-zone lecture he'd given himself on the drive to the restaurant.

Nine

Lia slid into a seat on the far right side of the sanctuary.

Maverick always sat in the center section near his family, so she stayed away from the middle seats altogether. Every breathing person in the congregation — and their brothers, uncles, cousins, and long-lost imaginary friends — thought she and Maverick should date. Sitting anywhere in his vicinity threw oil on that particular, combustible fire, so she avoided him like the plague at church.

Everyone knew the best way to remain friends with someone was to avoid being seen with them.

At least, that was how it worked when the two friends were of the opposite sex.

Lia chuckled. Even her mom thought she and Maverick should date. Her not-so-subtle hint-dropping was now in its third year.

Look at that Maverick. Bought his own home and he's not even thirty.

A stable man like Maverick is going to make some woman a fine husband one of these days.

I can picture Maverick with a couple of cute kids in tow. How many kids do you think you want?

If Lia couldn't get her own mom to understand she and Maverick weren't meant to be anything more than friends, then convincing other people was out of the question. Better to avoid him and bypass the whole discussion.

A blond ball of energy threw herself into the seat beside Lia. "I've missed you!" Watts wrapped her arms around Lia's neck and gave her a tight squeeze. "You're coming to lunch today, aren't you? I brought a surprise for you. You have to come. Tell me you're coming."

Lia resisted the urge to ruffle Watts' hair. What was acceptable when Maverick's sister had been eight, no longer went over particularly well in public. Hair ruffling was a thing of the past. Besides, they were in church, and she didn't need the other congregants to see her treating Watts like a little sister. The way her luck ran, people would get all kinds of crazy ideas from it.

The last time Watts had been home for church, she'd given Lia a herculean hug. The next day, the church's event coordinator had emailed to ask if she should reserve the church. For the Promise-Hoyt nuptials.

Nope. No hair ruffling today.

At least at church.

It would be fine later at the Hoyts' house. Lia had known Mr. and Mrs. Hoyt since her first grade year. They wouldn't get any weird ideas if she ruffled

Watts' hair. They were decent, solid, sensible people. Unlike her mother, who'd lost her last shred of sensibility when Lia had welcomed her twenty-eighth birthday without any marital prospects on the horizon.

"Lia, it's so good to see you!" Mrs. Hoyt pulled Lia into a hug and squeezed tight. "I see you every Sunday, but it's always from such a long distance. I miss visiting with you."

Guilt stabbed Lia's middle. "I know. It's just that... Um..."

The hug ended, but Mrs. Hoyt rested her hands on Lia's shoulders. "I know. Mav explained. You don't want people to think you're dating each other. Nobody's going to ask my opinion, but I think you could fix the whole problem by doing exactly what you don't want people to think you're doing. Date one another and get it over with."

"Wh-what?" Great. Now Mrs. Hoyt had jumped off the cliff, too. On the bright side, at least Lia's mother wouldn't be alone on the jagged rocks below.

"If avoiding him makes people think you're dating, maybe you should try dating him. Who knows? Maybe then people will think you're just friends."

The woman got an A for effort. The argument made sense. In an unhinged, kooky kind of way.

"Lia!" Watts came running up. "Come on, come on, come on. I have a surprise for you."

Maverick's younger sister tugged Lia out to the back patio. "Lia, meet Jacob and Wesley."

Lia peered from Watts to the two giant men standing by the outdoor grill. What on earth was that girl up to? "Nice to meet you."

One of the men looked like he'd rather crawl under a bed of nails than be stuck talking to her. The other had eyes that danced and twinkled in the noonday sun. Lia didn't know which was which, though. Watts hadn't bothered to elaborate before running off with a shout of, "Ferris!"

The smiling one quirked an eyebrow. "Ferris? Who's that?"

Lia waved in the general direction of the house. "Her brother."

"I thought Maverick was her brother."

"She has more than one."

He nodded before holding out his hand. "I'm Jacob, by the way. This one's Wesley."

Lia shook the proffered hands. Wesley had to be within spitting distance of twenty like Watts, while

Jacob outpaced them both by a good decade or so. "What brings you to the DC area?"

Wesley's face lit up like a Christmas tree, a bright red Christmas tree. Or maybe a stoplight.

Jacob tossed a glance at the younger man before shaking his head. "So her name's Watts. She has a brother named Maverick and another brother named Ferris?"

"And the Rottweiler you see sunning himself on the other side of the yard is Rambo Two."

"Two?"

"Yep."

"Was there a one?"

Maverick's scowl made its way into her line of sight as he moved across the lawn. "Um, yeah. He's in doggie heaven now."

Wesley found his voice. "I don't get it. What's the big deal with the names?"

Jacob grabbed a soda out of a nearby cooler and tossed it to Wesley. "You're too young. Don't worry about it." Then he gave his attention back to Lia. "For the record, I'm too young, too, but I grew up with a mess of older brothers."

"Brothers might explain how you recognize the names Maverick and Ferris. Even Rambo. But Watts? You're not secretly into chick flicks, are you?"

"Yeah, I sit up late at night with my pink slippers while I eat ice cream out of the tub and watch girl movies." He rolled his eyes. "So what is it with this family and the '80s?"

Jacob's puzzled expression brought a smile to Lia's face. "Mr. and Mrs. Hoyt love the '80s. They even used to have a cat named Buttercup."

"Let me guess. Kitty heaven?"

Lia chuckled. "Sadly, there was no sequel."

Jacob was still shaking his head when Maverick walked up and tapped Lia's elbow. "Can I have a word?"

Was he grinding his teeth? Lia nodded to Jacob and Wesley. "Please excuse me for a minute."

Maverick held the door for her, and Lia slipped into the house. When he shut the door and marched past her without speaking, however, she'd had enough. Lia spoke with the bluntness that a long friendship awarded her. "Either something's terribly wrong, or you're being terribly rude. I hope it's the former."

He got to the living room and pivoted to face her, the lines of his body taut. His face, normally open and friendly, was stiff, his lips drawn in a tight, bloodless line. "Do you realize what Watts brought them here for?"

Lia glanced over her shoulder for a second even though she couldn't see outside. "You mean Jacob and Wesley?"

"Who else would I be talking about?"

"Maverick, what's gotten into you? You're not acting like yourself. Did you get more word about your job?"

"She brought them to introduce to you. She's trying to fix you up."

"I'd really rather talk about your job." She wasn't clueless, but she'd kind of hoped everyone else would be.

He ran a hand through his hair and scowled at her. "Watts. Those men are from her squadron. They're paratroopers like her. She brought them to meet you. She's trying to find you a boyfriend. How can you not see that?"

Lia stared from Maverick to the wall that blocked her view of the back patio. "I know what she's doing. I just don't understand why."

"You mentioned your dating woes in some of your emails to her. She vetted the men in her squadron and picked a couple. She's planning on bringing them all here eventually so you can meet them and pick one."

Acid churned in her stomach. Someone she used to babysit was now trying to fix her up. Her life just hit a whole new level of pathetic. "What your sister is attempting to do is between me and her. Whether I like it or not is irrelevant. I'm not going to be rude—" She gave him a good glare. "—to those men out there just because I wish Watts didn't have an ulterior motive in inviting them."

"You should leave." Maverick waved her toward the front door.

"I want to catch up with Watts. She's my friend, and I haven't seen her in months."

"Fine." He bit out the single word before heading for the door himself. "I'm going for a walk. Tell Mom I'll be back in time for the food."

He was gone before Lia realized he genuinely meant to leave.

"Is everything all right in here?"

Lia circled to see Jacob standing in the open space between the living room and kitchen, hand tucked into his pockets. "I'm not sure. I think I missed something important."

He nodded toward the door Maverick had exited through. "He seems like an okay guy."

"He is. Usually."

Jacob gave her a solemn stare. "You didn't know Watts was trying to find a boyfriend for you?"

Lia felt the heat climbing into her cheeks. Curse her fair skin. "I might be the only one who didn't know."

He snorted. "Trust me. Wesley didn't know either. He only has eyes for Watts. As soon as he realized why we'd been invited for the weekend, he transformed from an affable guy into a sullen teenaged girl. Kind of like your friend Maverick."

"A teenaged girl? I'm pretty sure Maverick would take exception to that."

"Correct me if I'm wrong, but didn't he just go storming out the front door because you wouldn't leave this little get-together?"

He had a point.

"Take it from a guy. He didn't leave because he felt like taking a Sunday afternoon stroll. He left because you wouldn't."

On those parting words, he pushed himself off the wall and strode easily back through the kitchen and to the door that opened into the backyard.

He left because you wouldn't.

What did that even mean? She couldn't get a date to stick around, and now not even her best friend wanted to be around her?

With a sinking heart, Lia started toward the back door. The reflection in a mirror snagged her attention, though. She wasn't exactly looking her best today. She frowned as she forced her shoulders back and sucked her stomach in. It helped some, but not as much as she wanted. Was half a burger going to be a menu option at this meat-lovers' grill fest?

Ten

Maverick stomped his way up the steps to his parents' house. He cracked the front door open and let the silence wash over him before he crossed the threshold. Maybe everyone was so busy fawning over Watts and her friends that they hadn't paid any attention to his absence.

He made his way through the house and peeked out the kitchen door. They were all crowded around the patio table as they ate and laughed with one another. He would need to apologize eventually, but for now he hoped he could slip into the last open seat without too much fuss.

Of course, Lia sat between Ferris and one of the men Watts had dragged home with her.

Deep breath. He could do this.

Maverick pushed through the door, strode over to his mom, and leaned down to kiss her on the cheek. "Sorry I'm late. My short walk ended up being longer than I expected."

His mother frowned at him, worry in her eyes. "It's alright, dear. Sit down and get yourself some food."

He slid into the seat between his mother and the younger of Watts' two friends. "Which one are you?"

The man's gaze snapped to his, and for a second Maverick looked into a mirror. That boy was eaten up with jealousy. "Wesley."

Maverick followed Wesley's line of sight and couldn't decide if he was staring at Lia or at Watts. Maybe this weekend wouldn't be such a loss after all. "How did Watts convince you to come with her?"

The young man's jaw clenched. "By not telling me the real reason she dragged me along with her."

Maverick glanced back over at Watts. "Didn't realize she wanted to set you up with someone, huh?" It wasn't particularly Christian of him, but Wesley's irritation sure did brighten Maverick's outlook on life.

Wesley snorted. "Set up? Sure. Just not with a complete stranger old enough to be my…"

Maverick cleared his throat. "Careful there."

Wesley's ears became a vivid example of why the color fire-engine red belonged on fire trucks and not people. "You know what I mean."

Ha. Not only did Maverick understand what the kid meant, but he knew what he was going through, too. Jealousy. Pure and simple. "Does Watts have a clue how you feel?"

Wesley sputtered.

"The only way she'll know is if you tell her."

"She'll figure it out. She's smart."

Maverick almost wanted to smile. "The thing with women is that they have this reputation for being all intuitive and stuff, but they can be downright dense sometimes. You can wait for her to realize how you feel if you want, but you'll be waiting a long time."

Wesley's gaze cut to the side. "Nah. Watts is smarter than that. She's practically one of the guys."

Maverick tried to hide his laughter behind a cough. Wesley was in for a rude awakening.

Of course, that didn't say much for Maverick, either. He had zero intention of telling Lia about his outside-the-friend-zone thoughts. What was that word that described him? Oh yeah. It started with an *h* and ended with *ypocrite*.

"You're halfway to insane, and don't you dare try to tell me otherwise."

Maverick's baby sister had decided to help him wash dishes, and *that* was her conversation starter?

"Me? You jump out of airplanes for a living, and you're calling me crazy?"

Watts' eyes shone with her smile. "Can you believe it? I'm a paratrooper. Does life get any better than that?"

Maverick shook his head. "You're still a kid. You still have a lot of life left to live."

Watts waved her hand dismissively. "I can't imagine anything more fun than my life right now."

"Why are you meddling in Lia's life if yours is so perfect?"

His sister picked up a plate and began drying. "She sounded down in her last couple of emails. I wanted to help. Why were you such a jerk to her earlier?"

"Ouch." Leave it to Watts to spit out the truth like a mouthful of rusty nails. Of course she'd call him on it. She didn't do subtle.

"So?"

"It's complicated."

"Jumping out of an airplane at high altitudes is complicated. Being nice to someone who's been your friend since you were first potty trained shouldn't be."

"I had a rough week at work. And we haven't known each other that long."

"Since when does a bad week make it okay to be mean to people?" Watts should apply for a transfer. She needed to be a drill sergeant. "And you were what? Five when you met?"

"It doesn't. I'm going to apologize." He sighed. "We were six, not five."

Watts set the towel back down, the dishes only half-dried. "Make sure you follow through and tell her you're sorry because she's my friend too, and if you drive her away, she's not going to be the only one hurt."

His flighty baby sister had gone and turned into a woman of wisdom somewhere along the way. The whole world was topsy-turvy, and Maverick couldn't find his motion sickness pills.

Maverick sat in the booth and stared at the empty seat across from him. Lia wouldn't stand him up... would she? She'd left his parents' house before he could speak to her. The ER had been swamped all week, too. Every time he'd gone looking for her, she'd been running from one cubicle to another.

So he'd messed up last Sunday. That wasn't enough for her to write him off.

He glanced at the clock over the diner's front counter.

He'd even suffered through two dates so he would have something to tell Lia about, something that didn't involve his sudden preoccupation with her.

The clock read half past their normal meeting time. She would have texted to say she wasn't coming if she intended to bail on him. They'd had disagreements before, and she'd never gone AWOL. Unless he'd blown it even more than he thought.

Torn between ordering something and just leaving, Maverick reached for the sweetener packets. He should mix them all up so Lia would have something to do with her hands. She was happier when she could fidget.

"Sorry I'm late. I subbed in the nursery, and we had a visitor who about wanted to talk my ear off. I think she's been stuck at home with her new baby so long that she was desperate for adult conversation." Lia breezed into her usual seat. "Did you order, or were you waiting for me?"

Maverick pushed the sweetener packets aside. "You came."

"Was I not supposed to?" Her eyes dimmed.

"I thought my foul mood from last weekend might have scared you off."

She gave him a wink. "It takes more than one surly day to get rid of me." Lia picked up her menu, but before she started reading, she peeked over the top at him. "Did you hear the announcement about the mission trip this summer?"

Maverick stretched his arms out along the back of the booth. "Yeah. I'm thinking of doing it."

"Maybe that mission girl you dated would like to go with you."

He tapped his fingers on the table. "Nah. We're not seeing each other anymore. Besides, Alexa's heading off to a mission trip in the Ukraine later this month. What about you? Give it any thought yet?"

Lia's head angled to the side. "I wouldn't have even paid attention to the announcement if it wasn't for you going on that mission date. Now I kind of want to go."

"We could go together." Uh-oh. Wasn't that how he landed himself in the online dating nightmare that had become his life? He shook his head and opened his mouth to retract his words.

It was too late, though. Lia's eyes had already brightened. "You think so? If you're gonna do it, I'll sign up too. It'll be like the online dating." Color made its way up her neck as she chuckled. "Only more successful. We hope."

Someday he would learn to say no. Tomorrow was good enough. "Sure. Let's do it."

Her smile wiped away the last of his doubts. It would be a worthwhile trip. Serving God with a friend by his side? In a way, that defined the Christian walk.

Lia waved her hand in front of his face. "Where'd you go there?"

Maverick gave his head a small shake. "Got distracted by something shiny. What were you saying?"

"Did you get the email about the Holy Hearts fundraiser?"

He'd seen something in his inbox but hadn't paid attention. Maverick pulled his phone out to peruse his email while Lia scanned the menu. Why she read it was a mystery. She always ordered a salad.

"Huh." Holy Hearts had partnered with hospitals across the country in a fundraising effort designed to bring couples together while raising funds for medical needs. "A bachelor auction?"

Lia gave him a bright smile. "I signed up to help the day of the auction."

"Why a bachelor auction?"

She gaped at him as if he'd grown a second head. Or a third. "Because it's a fantastic way to raise money."

"Yeah, but… Why auction off men? Why not auction off women? Wouldn't that make even more money?"

Lia's head whipped from side to side. "No way. That's demeaning."

"So auctioning off a woman is demeaning, but auctioning off a man is perfectly acceptable?"

She gave him a pert nod. "Now you're catching on."

Maverick shook his head as the waitress approached. "What'll it be?"

"Double bacon cheeseburger, fries, and an extra side of bacon on the side."

The waitress angled her head toward Lia, pen poised.

"I'd like to try the…" She flipped the page of her menu. "Um…" She flipped another page. "This'll be on a separate check. Give me the hot turkey sandwich with a side of fruit instead of fries, please."

"Are you sure?" The waitress' eyebrow lifted.

Color climbed Lia's cheeks.

The waitress clucked her tongue. "Hot turkey sandwich with fruit. I'll have it out in a minute."

Maverick's knee started moving under the table. "So, did Mike ask you out yet?"

"Mike?"

"Single dad, cute kid."

"Mark, not Mike. How do you do that? You can't keep names straight, but you can remember all the technical computer mumbo jumbo words."

He waved the question away. "Whatever. Did he ask you out?"

Her shoulders slumped the tiniest bit. "He's decided to try another church."

"What does that have to do with dating?"

Lia slapped her hand down on the tabletop, drawing the eyes of neighboring patrons. "That's what I wondered. What if he's leaving the church to

95

avoid me? Is that my superpower now? Repelling eligible men? Is that why the singles' group has turned into an uninhabited wasteland?"

"He's an idiot."

Lia smiled. "He's not, but thanks for saying so."

Maverick swallowed. "I need to apologize."

Lia stared across the table, her grey eyes shining. "For what?"

"For last Sunday. And for making a big deal out of what you eat. It makes you uncomfortable, and I should stop."

She lifted one shoulder. "Last Sunday's forgiven. As for the food… It's something I struggle with. I didn't realize how much until you pointed it out to me."

"I can be dense sometimes, but not about this. You always look great. What's the struggle?"

Lia reached for the sweetener packets. "Did you know I had an eating disorder in high school?"

Her words pushed Maverick back into his seat. "No. How…? I don't…" He took a deep breath. "Want to tell me about it?"

The pink ones were all in order now. "There's not much to tell. The mirror showed me all the flaws. I never saw what was right. I saw all the excess body fat that needed to come off. So I'd skip meals and stuff. At the same time, it wasn't really about weight." She sighed and tucked a strand of hair behind her ear.

"I can give you the longer version or the short version."

He remembered Lia going through a skinny phase in high school, but he'd been busy with his other friends and life at the time, so he hadn't paid a ton of attention. As for excess body fat, she'd never had any as far as he could tell. Not that it mattered. Eating disorders were about perception more than reality if his memories of high school health class were serving him well. "I don't need the short version. I think my attention span can handle a long story if that's the one you want to share."

She exhaled slowly. "I had anorexia. If you ever read about it, you'll find out quick enough that anorexia is about control more than it is about weight. People whose lives are in chaos find something they can control, which often ends up being the food they eat. That's the easy explanation, I guess."

"So what was out of control in your life? What started it?"

"Remember Sally Simmons?"

"Yeah. She was your best friend in junior high, right?"

Lia nodded. "She moved away right as we started freshman year, and that made school really hard. Kind of lonely, too. Then my grandma died. It was all small stuff, and it's not like I thought, 'Oh, these bad things transpired, so now I'm going to control what I eat.' It just sort of happened."

The weight of Lia's words settled on Maverick's shoulders. She was trusting him with something immense. "I'm sorry I didn't know."

She gave him a half-smile. "You couldn't have. I hid it pretty well."

"How'd you get through it?"

She reached for the blue sweeteners. "My folks made me see a Christian counselor. I was ticked, but it's the best thing they could have done for me. He helped me to understand the things going on inside of me, things I wouldn't have ever figured out on my own. He reminded me, too, that the way God sees me is what really matters. Not just physically, but the whole picture. Sally moving away, Grandma dying, all of it. I felt like everything needed to be just so. I poured all my perfectionist tendencies into the one area of my life where I had control – what I ate. The thing is, God never asked me to be perfect, and He didn't ask me not to grieve Grandma or Sally. My feelings were okay with Him." She put the blue packets back. "I'm doing a really bad job of explaining."

Maverick reached out and rested his hand on Lia's. Her fidgety fingers stilled under his touch. "You're doing fine."

She turned her hand over and gave his a squeeze. "Anorexia is about body image, sure. But at the same time, it has nothing to do with body image. It's different for everybody. I used to count every single calorie, so I pay attention to those things. I knew if I ever started counting calories again, that I was in trouble."

"Have you been counting calories?"

"No, that's the problem. If I'd started doing that again, the red flag would have gone up, and I'd have realized I was in trouble. Only I wasn't, so it didn't, and I managed to fool myself into thinking everything was fine."

Talk about feeling out of control. Maverick might as well have been thrown into the ocean without a life preserver. "You switched to salads after Plus-Size Jerk."

She reached for the yellow packets. "Not exactly. I switched before then. You just didn't notice until him. I was fine at first, but when the dates kept going so wrong, I… I guess I kind of forgot some of the stuff I'd worked so hard to learn back in high school."

He nodded toward her plate. "So what changed? What made you realize you were getting back into dangerous territory?"

"You."

"Me?" She couldn't have knocked the wind out of him any better if she'd gut-punched him. "What did I do?"

She tucked the sugar packets back into their black rectangular container and pushed it to the side.

"You offered to use brass knuckles on a guy who made a comment about my weight."

"I wouldn't have actually…"

Lia cut him off. "Well, duh. But still… Even without the brass knuckles, you knocked some sense into me. You forced me to take a look at myself and realize how weird I'd gotten about my food again and how critical I was being of my own body. I mean, I was wounded whenever another person judged me based on appearance, but I was doing the same thing to myself. How crazy is that?"

"Are you going back to counseling?" He hurt for her, but they were way outside his comfort zone. What if he said the wrong thing?

She knotted her fingers together. "I have an appointment for next week. It's mostly for accountability, though. I have all the tools to deal with this, but it helps if I know someone else is watching me, too."

Maverick wanted nothing more than to pull her into a tight hug and never let go. "The sandwich is a nice change."

She offered him a wry grin. "I was so sick of lettuce. You have no idea."

Eleven

Lia hadn't felt this light in a long time. Not in body, but in spirit. The whole weight thing had snuck up on her. If Maverick hadn't gone and made such a stink about what she ate, she never would have realized she'd slipped back into old ways. He always managed to poke at the soft spots on her soul without meaning to.

She was always a better person for it, too. Not that she'd ever tell him so.

Maverick was good for her. Good to her, too. Some woman would be very blessed to capture his heart and call him husband.

"So tell me about your dates this week. Fun, funny, or disastrous?"

He looked like he wanted to say more about her revelation, but the waitress picked that exact moment to deliver their food.

She set Lia's plate down with a gentler-than-usual *thunk*. "Whenever I order the hot turkey sandwich, I always have them put bacon on it, too. Something about that combination…" Their normally taciturn waitress never talked that much.

Maverick lifted an eyebrow, and Lia nodded. He slid the extra bacon from his plate over to hers as the waitress retreated. Then he bowed his head. "Lord, thank you for the food, for our server, and for the cooks in the back. Thank you for our day of rest, for the blue sky outside, and for Lia. Continue to strengthen her in mind, body, and spirit, Lord, and help her see herself as You see her. Amen."

Warmth pooled in her middle as Lia echoed his *amen*. God had really done something special when He'd given her Maverick for a friend. She reached for her knife and fork, ready to tackle the challenge in front of her. "Come on. You're not getting out of it that easy. Your dating life?"

He took a huge bite of his burger before setting it back down. He held up two fingers as he swallowed. "Two dates this week. Shondra and Leann."

"And?"

"Shondra was nice. We caught a matinee and had lunch. We might go out again. I'm not sure either of us is feeling it, but we didn't have a terrible time together."

"Ha. So that's the criteria for getting a second date with you? Not to give you a terrible first date?" Lia chuckled. "Way to set the bar high. So what about Leann?"

"You know how I chose not to have my picture show?"

She nodded.

"I wanted people to get to know me for who I am." He gave a half-shrug. "Besides, let's face it. I'm a computer geek. It's not like I'm ripped or anything."

"So what happened?"

Maverick rolled his eyes. "I thought when women hid their picture, it would be for the same reasons. They want to be judged for who they are and not what they look like. You know, avoid the whole objectification thing."

"Eh." Lia gave him points for trying. "Some women might do it for that reason. Others hide theirs for different reasons."

"Yeah. I kind of figured that part out."

Lia took another bite of her sandwich. "You're killing me here. What did Leann look like?"

"White."

"White? You mean Caucasian? Because if so, aren't you white too?"

Maverick shook his head. "No. I mean white. W. H. I. T.E."

"I'm not following."

"Leann's a mime. She showed up in white face paint and didn't speak during the entire meal. She pantomimed everything. I think at one point she may have told me I reminded her of a rusty boat shaped like a baby elephant, but I can't be certain. Apparently, I'm not up-to-date on mimery."

Lia swallowed the last bite of her sandwich and reached for her fruit bowl. "Is that even a word?"

"Hey, if you'd been on that date, then you'd have earned the privilege of making up whatever words you wanted. You weren't there, though. I was. So the word-making-up privileges are all mine."

"Fair enough." She popped a grape into her mouth. "Did Leann meet the standard to earn a second date, or is that bar too high for her?"

Maverick leaned his head back. "You think I'm being unreasonable?"

"Oh no. Definitely not." Lia slid her fork into a piece of cantaloupe. "Communication is vital to any relationship. You have to speak the same language, or it's going to be tough. Either you need to learn mimery, or she needs to use flashcards. Otherwise the relationship's doomed."

"Ha. See? Mimery."

Lia picked up another grape.

"So what about you? Any hot dates this week?" His left eyebrow lifted with the question.

She felt the heat climb her cheeks. "Well, there was the whole thing with Watts trying to set me up with not one, but two of her fellow paratroopers. One of which watched Watts like a lovesick puppy every time she crossed his path."

"And the other?"

"Decent enough guy, but I don't think I'm cut out to be a military wife. Not right now, anyway. I suppose if God wanted me to marry someone in the military, I would, and I'd trust Him to change my heart about it. But for now? Nah. I don't see that in my future."

The corner of Maverick's mouth tipped up, which made no sense. She hadn't said anything funny.

"Aside from that, I did go out yesterday afternoon with a guy from Holy Hearts."

The corner of his mouth dipped back down. "Name?"

"Baldric."

"That's a weird name."

"He's Australian. Great accent."

"Is that where you set your bar for a second date? You have to like the guy's speaking voice?"

Lia chuckled. "Nah. I have to like his voice and his hairstyle."

"What about Baldric's hair?"

"Didn't have any."

Maverick's eyes widened. "Oh no. Please don't tell me he listed his name as Bald Rick and you misread it for Baldric."

Lia couldn't have stopped the laughter if she'd wanted to. "You're never going to let me live down that whole Network Elf thing, are you?"

He shook his head. "Not anytime soon."

She swallowed the last bite of honeydew and set her fork down. "His name is actually Baldric, and yes, he's bald, but it's not related to his name."

"If you say so."

"He's still not getting a second date."

"Why not?"

"Mm… He was a little too touchy-feely. Kind of gave me the creeps."

"He doesn't know where you live, does he?"

Lia shook her head. "Online Dating 101, remember? Never tell them where you live or work."

"Or attend church."

She nodded. "That too."

A comfortable silence settled between them before Maverick spoke up. "So he pretty much did his talking with his hands, too, huh?"

Lia wadded up her napkin and threw it at him.

Lia got to the restaurant early and took a seat. She pulled out her phone and opened the Holy Hearts app. It couldn't hurt to see if she had any HeartGrams waiting for her.

Rod would arrive soon. She still hadn't figured out what he did for a living in the computer industry, but he'd come across as kind each time he'd messaged.

A quick look at her Holy Hearts dashboard told her the other two men she'd contacted back when she first reached out to Rod had never gotten back to her. Community Support Specialist Michael never replied and Firefighter Zeke, the one she'd been most interested in, had disappeared. His profile was no longer active on Holy Hearts. Maybe he'd found someone and was working on his happily ever after.

She slipped her phone back into her purse as someone approached her table.

"You're Lia, right?"

She nodded to him. "Rod?"

He slid into the seat across from her and held out his hand. "Nice to meet you."

They shook hands, and Lia put on her welcoming smile. "So how has your day been so far?"

"Fair to middling, but it's looking up now."

Be still her heart, his eyes actually twinkled when he smiled. "Why don't you tell me about it?"

"I work at a small computer company. We address the networking and security needs of small businesses. It's usually mundane, but today one of our clients had a network malfunction."

Lia winced. "Let me guess. The client didn't call to ask for your help. He called to blame you for the problem?"

Rod waggled his hand. "He started the day irate, but ended the day with an apology, so we'll call that one a win."

"I have a friend who works in IT at a local hospital. He tells some of the funniest stories about the people who end up with computer problems. He says some of the staff should be permanently barred from ever being in the same room with a computer terminal."

"I feel his pain. The worst is when there's a tiny little problem — something not even related to the network — but then they try to fix that tiny little problem and cause the whole network to crash. Then you're getting chewed out for something they did."

Lia chuckled. "Tell me about your most ridiculous call, the one you tell all the newbies to warn them and make them laugh at the same time."

Rod sat back in his chair and thought for a minute. "We'd worked with this one company from the time they were ten employees strong on up until they had over five hundred employees. We knew the CEO well, although as the company grew, we no longer heard from him when they needed help. The calls started coming from a receptionist or a Vice President of Such-and-Such. Until one day, I got a call at two in the morning on my personal cell phone from Mr. CEO. He was livid. The network was down, and it was the day they were supposed to be taking the company public. He threatened to sue me for millions."

"Ouch."

"Needless to say, I dragged my entire team out of their beds and rushed down to his offices."

He paused, and Lia leaned forward. "And?"

Rod shook his head. "Someone had installed an update to the operating system, and as a result, the color scheme for his desktop had changed. The CEO didn't like the new colors, but instead of calling their tech guy to change the color scheme back, he went into the Control Panel settings, and in the process of poking around, he disconnected his computer from the network."

Lia shook her head. "My friend Maverick would love this story. He deals with doctors, and no matter how smart they might be in their chosen field, when it comes to computers, some of them are beyond clueless. So what happened with the CEO?"

"He was all bluster that day. I understood. The whole IPO thing was huge for him and his family. A couple days later, though, after the craziness had died down, he called me up — at a reasonable hour —and asked if he could contract with our company to provide someone on-site to maintain the network."

"Why didn't he just hire his own network guy?"

Rod shrugged one shoulder. "I think the contract offer was his apology. Men don't always come out and say the words."

Lia reached for the water glass the waitress had placed in front of her. "So what'd you do? Take the contract or say 'Good riddance'?"

"We agreed to a two-year contract with the caveat that if he chose not to renew in two years, he would pay us to find the right person for his company and to get them up to speed."

"Hopefully he made it well worth your while?"

"It was an advantageous move for us, and having our name linked to his company has brought us a lot of business."

After another similar story, Lia glanced at the clock on her phone. "Wow. Has it really been two hours? I hate to bring this to an end, but I should get going."

Rod nodded to her, and the smile in his eyes said it had been an enjoyable evening.

Whew. She'd needed a dating win.

He helped her on with her coat. "I'd like to see you again if that's okay with you."

"I'd like that, too." He bit his lip, and the dating win began to slip from Lia's grasp. "What's on your mind?"

Rod held the restaurant's front door open for her. When they were out on the sidewalk, he met her gaze. "I'm going to be out of town for a couple of weeks on a business trip, but I'll send you a HeartGram when I return."

"Okay…?" She let the question hang between them and waited for him to add the "but" she could sense coming.

"Can I be blunt?"

And now the dating win began circling the drain. "I suppose."

"You told almost as many stories about your friend Maverick tonight as you did yourself. It makes me wonder if there's more to your relationship than you're saying. I enjoyed the evening, and I'd like to do it again, but there's no point if you're already involved with someone else."

"We're just friends." Lia would have shaken her head to emphasize the point, but somehow she didn't think it would help. Why was Rod so preoccupied with her and Maverick's friendship?

"Then maybe there's more to it than you're telling yourself. Either way, give it some thought. I'll let you know when I'm back in town. If you've decided by then that your affection belongs elsewhere, I'll understand. Just tell me straight." He leaned in then and brushed his lips against her cheek. "I really did have a wonderful time, and I hope you did, too."

Of course she had. Right up until he'd mentioned Maverick. And the kicker? Rod seemed like a genuinely good guy. She'd enjoyed their dinner and the conversation they'd shared.

Sigh.

Goodbye dating win.

A couple days later, IT got called down to the ER again. More network troubles. They could pull up medical histories on most of their patients, but not all. It seemed either random or specific — she wasn't sure which. This time two men Lia didn't recognize accompanied Maverick. She gave him a quick wave but didn't have a chance to stop and talk to him. With his new shadows, it was probably for the best anyway.

Partway through the morning, Lia rushed out of Cubicle 7C only to run smack dab into the more daunting of her friend's shadows. "Pardon me." She tried to skirt around him to reach the computer workstation, but he blocked her path.

"Can I have a word with you?"

She shook her head. "I need to enter something into the computer. You'll have to follow me if you want to talk."

The man fell into step beside her as she headed to the closest workstation. "Name's Whitehall. I'm with the Secret Service."

Talk about a weird name. Who named their kid Whitehall?

"It's Agent Whitehall."

Secret Service agent *and* mind reader. How'd he know she'd thought Whitehall was his first name?

"What interest do the feds have in our network issues?"

"That's classified, ma'am."

Lia reached the workstation and flicked her gaze at the agent. "Let me see your ID, and don't call me Ma'am. Lia or Nurse Promise is fine."

Agent Whitehall showed her his credentials. They looked legitimate. Not that she'd know a forgery if she saw one.

He tucked his ID back into his jacket pocket. "Have you seen anybody working at the workstations in the ER that shouldn't be here?"

Lia logged into the system. "Nope. But we're always so busy in here, I'm not sure any of us would notice someone at one of the workstations."

Agent Whitehall frowned. "So you're saying any Joe Schmoe off the street could walk in and access one of your computer workstations?"

She shook her head. "A patient accessing a workstation would draw attention. If someone came in through the hospital entrance, though, and acted like they belonged, we wouldn't give it a second thought. Some of us might look long enough to make sure the person had an ID badge, but I doubt any of us would take the time to go over and read the badge and ensure it was legit. Why?"

"How many ways are there to get into the ER?"

Lia frowned as she typed the patient stats into the workstation. The network problem had also messed with their ability to enter information from their assigned tablets. "To get into the bullpen, you either come in from the ER waiting room, or you use one of the two hospital entrances, both of which require you to swipe a badge."

"What about linens? How are your linens stocked?"

"The hospital contracts that out. They come every day, pick up the soiled linens and restock our shelves with fresh ones."

"And how do they get in?"

"They have to swipe in like everybody else."

"Any other outside contractors that can swipe themselves into the ER?"

"Sure." Lia bit her bottom lip as she tried to remember. "The people who collect the sharps containers are contracted out. There's some sort of service that comes in periodically to check all the smoke detectors and fire extinguishers. We get bureaucrats from time to time who have to check us out to make sure we can keep our accreditation. Sometimes we have to bring in counselors from a palliative care facility. We don't deal with that much in the ER. People are usually admitted to the hospital before anybody like that is called in, but it happens occasionally. And the paramedics who bring in patients via ambulance. " She shrugged. "I'm sure there are others, but I can't think of them at the moment."

Agent Whitehall shook Lia's hand. "Thanks for your time." He started to walk away then turned around and asked, his voice casual, "Do you know Mr. Hoyt?"

Lia didn't lift her eyes from the workstation's computer screen. "Maverick? We go to the same church. We've known each other since we were kids."

The agent nodded. "Is he a trustworthy sort?"

Lia's spine stiffened. Was the world conspiring against her? Now complete strangers were asking her about her friend. "Maverick Hoyt is a man who does what's honorable even when it comes at a personal cost to himself."

Agent Whitehall nodded. "That's what I thought. Just wanted a second opinion. Thanks."

Before Lia cold think of anything else to say in Maverick's defense, the agent was gone. Come to think of it, Maverick and his other shadow were gone, too.

What exactly was going on? Lia wasn't prone to conspiracy theories, but the problems with the hospital's network were becoming more bizarre by the minute. Secret Service of all things. Why would they care about a private hospital's network?

Unless...

Twelve

Call me when you get a chance. I have a question.

Maverick read the text again as he walked in through his front door.

He and Lia texted sometimes during the week, but they rarely chatted on the phone. They saw enough of each other in person that there'd never been much of a need.

Something must be wrong.

Maverick scrolled through his contacts list, found Lia, and tapped *Call*.

"Hey." Lia's voice sounded normal enough.

"What's up?"

"Who were the guys with you in the ER today?"

"Butch Hutchinson. He's the head of the cybersecurity team Ferito Technology sent to ferret out the hacker who's compromised our network. The other guy was someone he brought in. Whitehall, I think. I didn't catch his title, though."

"Secret Service."

"Huh?"

Lia grunted. "Agent Whitehall. He's with the Secret Service."

"How do you know that?"

"He asked me some questions, but he showed me his credentials first."

"Secret Service?"

"Right?" Lia's voice went up in pitch. "It got me to thinking. Why would the Secret Service care about our computer problems at the hospital? Then it hit me. Remember the assassination attempt?"

Maverick toed his shoes off before padding into the kitchen in search of a cold bottle of water. "That was a year ago. What does that have to do with now?"

Lia's sigh sounded like a long slide down on a bass trombone. "Jefferson David Taylor was running for the republican nomination when he got shot. He was basically a nobody back then."

"Not a nobody, but yeah. What're you getting at?"

"He was treated in our ICU."

"Okay…"

"Hello? He's president now. For Secret Service to show up, they must think an attack on the hospital's network is somehow a threat to national security. Like the president…?"

"They probably don't want the president's private medical records to fall into the wrong hands. It could be a matter of privacy, not national security."

"I like my explanation better. What if Taylor has some crazy disease that's reported in our hospital records? Or what if…"

Maverick cut her off. "What if someone wants to make it look like something's wrong with him? What if someone is attempting to isolate patient records so they can tamper with them?"

Lia grunted. "Can someone do that with the port thingy you mentioned? The one that got turned off?"

He cringed. *Port thingy? Really?* "The fact that the port was shut down via software means it was hacked. For someone to get in there and control that port kind of means they own it, that they can do whatever they want with it. They'd need to have some mad computer skills to pull that off, but once they took ownership of the ER router port, it would have given them a doorway to hack further into the system."

"Like patient records?"

"Maybe. I'd like to think we cut them off before they got that far, but this problem has been going on for a while. It's hard to know how far they got or what they accessed. The cybersecurity team is still working on that, trying to trace the digital fingerprints through the system"

Lia's brow wrinkled. "Yeah, but every time a patient record is accessed, it's timestamped and the person who accessed it is recorded, too. So wouldn't it be easy to know?"

Maverick tapped the side of his head. "Mad computer skills, remember? If they took ownership of the port, then they're good enough to take ownership of the security software that monitors the patient records. Which is why I think it makes more sense that they'd try to make his records look like something's wrong with him. If they just wanted to get a peek at his records, there are easier ways to do that. Making it look like the president's sick, though, and then releasing those records to the public? That could cause major problems. Economy, foreign relations, you name it."

"Okay, fine. That makes more sense than my theory. Perception is everything, right? If they can make people think the president's not fit to serve…" Lia sat back. "You should ask Agent Whitehall if he shows up again."

"That's above my pay grade."

"He asked me about you."

Maverick settled on his couch and stretched his legs out, resting his feet on the coffee table. Agent Whitehall had… "He what?"

"Agent Whitehall asked what I thought of you. Were you trustworthy, that sort of thing."

"What'd you tell him?"

"The truth, silly. That your word can be trusted even if you have zero talent as a mime."

Maverick leaned his head back. "It's all a little too weird for me. Doing IT work at a hospital used to be straightforward and simple. Interesting, yeah, but not weird."

Lia threw a bucket of cold water in his face with her next words. "I signed you up for the bachelor auction."

Maverick sputtered and sat bolt upright. "You what?"

"The auction proceeds are designated to help fund the Child Life Department. It's for Child Life. You wouldn't have been able to say no, so I put your name down."

"I can't say no because you didn't give me a chance. And I thought it was supposed to fund equipment."

"Pish posh. You were going to give in eventually. I just saved you all the waffling between now and auction day. It's easier this way. As for the money, different departments submitted proposals. Rylie's Child Life proposal impressed the board the most, I guess. I wouldn't be surprised if guilt played a part, too, with the way they've cut funding to Child Life."

Maverick let out a deep sigh. "I still don't understand what Holy Hearts gets from this. I see how the hospital benefits, but a dating service? What's in it for them?"

"All the men being auctioned off have to be single and have to create a profile on Holy Hearts. That way the women coming to the auction will see all the great-looking doctors and whatever on stage and will think Holy Hearts has all the best men. Business should boom."

"That sounds kind of mercenary for what's supposed to be a Christian company."

"Yeah, I'm guessing. Maybe it really is a charity thing, no ulterior motive. Like you said, they're a Christian dating service. What if the whole auction thing is about paying it forward and doing good for others? They might not have a hidden agenda."

Maverick shook his head. "In business, there's always an ulterior motive."

"Aren't you a ray of sunshine tonight?"

"Ha. Funny. So what's the dress code for this meat market you're calling a bachelor auction? Do I need to rent a tux?"

Lia's light laughter floated across the airwaves. "We're going for something a little more informal. You'll see an announcement in your Holy Hearts email soon. It should answer all your questions."

"Why do I get the feeling I should avoid opening email for the foreseeable future?"

Her voice held a smile. "You're coming whether you like it or not, so try to be a sport."

Maverick's body was having dinner with Vanessa, a woman he'd met through Holy Hearts. His mind, however, wasn't even in the same building with her.

Snapping fingers drew his attention. "I'm sorry. What did you say?"

"Look." Vanessa rose from the table and put her hands on her trim hips. "If you're not into me, that's fine. I knew you weren't looking for marriage here. You made that clear. Friends only. Whatever. I don't want anything serious, either, but I'd like to meet a guy who's stable enough that I can take him to the company Christmas party without having to file a disclaimer with HR at the end of the evening."

She realized it was only spring, didn't she? Christmas was so far in the future it belonged in a sci-fi movie.

Vanessa huffed. "I don't need your undying love, but expecting you to be present, here with me in this conversation is not asking too much."

He'd blown it. Again. Maverick ran a hand over his face. "I'm sorry Vanessa. My distraction isn't about you."

"You think I don't know that? Whatever her name is, you either sort it out, or move on. But stop wasting everybody else's time."

Maverick didn't try to halt her as Vanessa stomped away from the table. She had every reason to be angry. Instead, he lifted his hand to the waiter and indicated he was ready for the check. The waiter humored him with a nod of acknowledgment even though everyone in the restaurant knew he was done with his date. Vanessa had been far from quiet in her complaints.

Once the waiter returned with the check, Maverick paid the bill, collected his jacket, slipped outside into the darkening twilight, and headed toward the parking garage on the other side of the street. He and Vanessa had driven separately, so at least he didn't have to worry about her trying to hail a cab. Where guilt should be gnawing at him, he felt relief. Lia's question from weeks prior came back to him. Were women who made the first move aggressive? No, not normally. Vanessa, on the other hand... He had a feeling she would have chewed him out no matter how their date had gone.

The *walk* signal lit up, and Maverick stepped onto the asphalt. He hit the halfway mark in the crosswalk before the yelling registered. Someone was calling his name. "Hoyt! Hey, Hoyt!"

Not many men addressed him by his last name. Maverick made his way across the rest of the street, stepped up onto the curb, and glanced around until he spotted the face that went with the voice. "What can I do for you Agent Whitehall?"

"Nice little scene back there."

Maverick stared at the agent. "Are you stalking me now?"

"Nah. You wouldn't know I was here if that was the case. I'm stealthy like that. Now let me buy you a beer."

"No, thanks."

"Please tell me you're not a wine guy."

Maverick shook his head. "I'm not much of an alcohol guy — wine, beer, or otherwise."

"Coffee then." Whitehall pointed down the street to an exclusive coffee bistro Maverick recognized by name but had never braved entering.

"As long as you're buying. And I think you have to be on the VIP list. I heard they have an actual bouncer."

Whitehall gave a solemn nod. "I know a guy who knows a guy."

Within minutes, they were seated at a corner table. A barista approached with her order pad at the ready, but before she could speak, Agent Whitehall rattled off the names of a couple drinks. "Give me a Dolley Madison Zebra, hot, and get my friend here a Bess Truman Puñet, also hot."

Maverick had no idea what a puñet was. A drink named after the wife of America's thirty-third president couldn't be all bad, though… he hoped.

The instant their barista stepped away, Whitehall leaned forward, elbows resting on the tabletop's edge in defiance of every etiquette lesson ever taught. "Tell me what you think of Planter."

The agent had followed him after a restaurant altercation to ask what he thought of his supervisor. Could the night get any more bizarre? "He's my boss. What I think of him doesn't matter."

Something flickered in Whitehall's eyes. Humor, maybe admiration. Or gas. Wasn't that what they said when babies smiled?

"Fair enough. Hutchinson, then. What do you think of him?"

He could answer that one honestly without risking termination. Hopefully. "He's an analytical person who notices things even though he doesn't want people to know he's paying attention. He's smarter than he wants others to realize, but he's not the type to play dumb."

"Is he any good at his job?"

Maverick sat back as the barista set a drink in front of him. He picked it up and took a sip, still not sure he trusted what Whitehall had ordered for him. The rich coffee ran over his tongue, bringing a contented sigh to his lips. He should find an excuse to answer questions for Whitehall more often if this was how the guy rewarded people for their cooperation. "I don't know."

"You've been working with him. How can you not know?"

He took another swallow of his coffee. "He's great at what I've seen him do, but his job is a whole lot bigger than one little hospital network. I can't speak to any of the rest of what he does."

Whitehall nodded and downed half his coffee. "What about you? How are you at your job?"

Why did this suddenly feel like an interrogation? "I'm better at it than some, not as skilled as others."

"You don't give yourself enough credit. You graduated at the top of your class, didn't you?"

"Sure, but classroom knowledge and experience are two different things, and in a field that's changing constantly, the experience pays off way more than anything I learned in a textbook."

"Are you ever going to ask that nurse out?"

Intrusive much? "My personal life is none of your business."

"The redhead, right? You should ask her out before she finds someone else."

Maverick ground his teeth together.

"She's a looker alright. Good at her job, too. I did some checking."

Maverick thought about throwing the rest of his coffee at Whitehall, but the drink was too good for that. What else could he throw? The table didn't even have a napkin dispenser on it. The place could afford a bouncer but not weaponry for the tables? What a waste.

Whitehall tossed a twenty down onto the table and slid out of the booth. "I enjoyed our little chat. Take your time finishing the coffee."

Maverick took a sip of the drink in question, but the velvety smooth flavor of a moment ago was gone. It tasted like chalk. Either that, or the agent's questions about Lia had pushed all his buttons.

Maverick headed back into the crisp night air. Who exactly was Agent Whitehall, anyway? And why was he poking his nose into Maverick's business?

Thirteen

"Promise!"

Lia's head snapped up at the sound of her last name being yelled. Dr. Zagel was on duty today. That meant the chances of her getting a real lunch break were slim to none. Good thing she'd managed a bowl of oatmeal for breakfast.

She took a deep breath and jogged toward the doctor. "Where do you need me?"

"Show Johnson how to suture or that woman in there's going to end up looking like Frankenstein."

Mallory Johnson was the trainee who'd ended up with blood in her mouth following a botched IV attempt. At least she hadn't given up on the job after that incident. It helped that the patient's bloodwork had all been clean. It would all be for nothing, though, if Dr. Z kept after her like he was doing.

Lia unclenched her jaw. "Frankenstein's monster."

"What?" Dr. Zagel's eyebrows drew together like two hairy moths toward an invisible flame.

"Frankenstein was the doctor, not the monster."

His eyes widened, and color climbed his neck. Dr. Zagel wasn't used to being questioned, let alone corrected. Before the building steam could erupt, Lia slipped away from him and into cubicle 6B. "How's it going in here?"

The cubicle's curtain barely provided privacy. Blocking out sound was beyond impossible. So it was no surprise that Johnson stood with her needle half in and half out of a woman's right cheek while the patient's wide eyes and chalky-white skin spoke of her terror. Somebody needed to teach Dr. Z some bedside manners, or, if nothing else, how to whisper.

Lia stepped up to the foot of the bed and looked the patient in the eyes. "Nurse Johnson here is doing a fabulous job. Ignore Dr. Zagel. He wasn't hugged enough as a child. You're in great hands."

Mallory started moving the needle again, completing that suture and progressing to the next. Her hands shook, but her stitch work was solid, so Lia kept up her meant-to-be-soothing monologue.

"You're going to be swollen for a while, and your face is going to look rough. Once the swelling goes down and the stitches are removed, it'll get better. You can come back to the ER to get your stitches out, or you can go to your family physician. Either way, just be sure to ask for suggestions about how to minimize any scarring. There are a lot of miracle-working topical ointments on the market. You don't want to apply any of those until you're healed, though. Otherwise they could hurt more than they help."

Nurse Johnson got the last suture into place and tied off. "There you go, Miss Hampton. All done with the suturing. The doctor will want to come back in and take a peek. In the meantime, I'll print out your paperwork so you can go home."

Johnson stepped out of the cubicle, Lia on her heels. "Thank you."

"We've all been new before, and we've all gotten on Dr. Zagel's bad side. Don't worry about it. Go start the paperwork, and I'll let him know the suturing's complete."

Nurse Johnson headed off toward the printer as she tapped information into her tablet. Lia circled around and scanned the bullpen for Dr. Zagel's distinct hairstyle.

Aha! The overgrown black pompadour — which Dr. Z claimed was a rebellion against the haircut he'd had in the Army — bobbed up and down as the doctor berated a technician. "The suturing's done in 6B. Did you want to examine the work, or should we release her?"

His head snapped up, his eyes darker than usual. "I want to see it." Without bothering to finish his complaint against the technician, the doctor headed toward 6B. Lia jogged to keep up. Something sure had gotten itself stuck in Dr. Zagel's craw. He always held everyone to his exacting standards, but today was worse than normal. A standing joke in the nurse's locker room was whether or not Dr. Z was wearing his cranky pants. His present attitude, though, made cranky pants seem like sunshine and daisies. What had he put on today? His ogre pants? Angry pants? Meany pants? None of them did his current mood justice.

Lia arrived at 6B as Johnson approached from the other side and the doctor stepped back out of the cubicle. He shook a finger at the trainee. "You need to learn to suture like Promise here. That's skillful work. I hope you paid attention."

He stormed off in search of his next victim while Johnson's stare moved from Lia to the curtained cubicle. "He thinks you did it?"

"Not on purpose. I couldn't keep up with him. He was already coming out by the time I got here."

Johnson's face split in a grin. "Are you kidding me? I don't care if he knows I put in the sutures. He thinks you did it. Every time I've done something that didn't meet Dr. Z's expectation, he's told me I should pay more attention to you. And he thinks the work in there is yours. My day is made. My whole week, for that matter."

Lia grinned at the younger nurse. "Glad I could help."

"Do I get to see this fancy stitch work anytime soon?" The voice came from within the cubicle. "Or are you too busy congratulating yourself out there?"

Lia gave Mallory a shove toward the cubicle before heading back across the bullpen to the patient she'd left in order to help with the stitches, but a nagging thought took the usual bounce from her step. The suturing was good enough for Dr. Z only because he believed Lia had done the work. Why did that bother her so much?

That night when Lia got home, she pulled up her Holy Hearts profile and examined it. The time had come to make some changes. The scene with Dr. Zagel had haunted her all day until she'd finally realized why it continued to nag at her subconscious.

The stitching was adequate only because he thought she'd done it. It was a silly, small thing. Yet it spoke to everything she was struggling with in her own heart.

Appearances were more important than they should be. What people thought they saw influenced their thinking as much as what they actually saw. She wasn't sure how that fit into the dating world, but Lia was certain about one thing. It was time to block her picture. If people wanted to reach out to her — or respond to her HeartGrams — fine. She was tired of ending up on dates with men, though, whose first words were about how they'd always dreamed of dating a redhead.

Lia changed a couple of other things while she was in her profile, too. Then she sat back, studied her new pictureless profile, and took a deep breath. She could do this. She could *not* care about appearances — hers or anyone else's. Which meant she needed to consider men without pictures. She'd always responded to them when they reached out to her, but she'd never initiated contact with any. A new outlook on dating, though, would be wasted if she wasn't willing to try some new things.

The photographs people used weren't always honest, anyway. Take Baldric, for example. His picture showcased a full head of hair. Or — shudder — the Network Elf. His picture clearly predated his couch potato days.

Nope. Pictures often lied. Better to start going with profiles that didn't show one. Less opportunity for dishonesty that way.

Lia glanced through a handful of the profiles before sending off a short message to two who interested her. Maybe it would turn into something. There was only one way to find out.

For the first time since she'd started on this whole online quest, she wasn't drowning in dating stress. She savored the anxiety-free moment and appreciated it like the gift it was.

When she took a step back and looked, she had to admit her life was pretty fantastic. She loved her job, her family, her friends, and her church. Her days were full even if her nights sometimes felt lonely.

She snapped the computer closed and headed into her bathroom to take a shower. Before she reached for the knob, she stopped and peered at herself in the mirror. She had a few more lines around her eyes than most women her age. Dad said it was because she had an easy laugh. He also said her future husband would find those lines attractive. Mom said she should use more moisturizer.

Lia leaned close to the mirror and tugged the skin tight around her eyes. It made her look like a fish, but it didn't miraculously make her face any younger. And she was fine with that. Hm.

Her counselor believed her problem with food had started back up, not because she'd been unhappy with her appearance, but because she'd been afraid no one would love her for who she was on the inside. She didn't agree with him, but she didn't disagree, either.

She knew who she was in Christ, and He loved her. He was enough for her. So why did she continue to seek more? Even when they were wrong, why did she let the comments of her dates burrow so deeply into her soul? It defied logic.

But then, eating disorders in general weren't always rational. They were in a twisted makes-sense-at-the-time kind of way. When the light of common sense shined on them, though, it became apparent eating disorders were a symptom that rarely seemed to fit the actual problem. Just look at her. She was a nurse, for pity's sake. She understood the importance of nutrition and a balanced diet. Yet there she was, struggling to put the monster of anorexia back in its box. She might be able to excuse her behavior when she was a kid, but she was all grown up now.

Which in a strange way brought her full circle and back to the question she'd started with. Why had she reverted to old habits and ways of thinking when she so clearly knew better?

She hadn't figured out why yet, but she would get to the heart of the matter eventually. In the meantime, she was making sure she ate nutritious meals, and she'd hidden her profile picture. She smiled at her reflection. She'd have put her photo under lock and key ages ago if she'd known how freeing it would be.

It might feel like baby steps to someone else, but for her, those two changes were huge.

Lia hummed as she started the shower.

Fourteen

Maverick eyed his Holy Hearts inbox. He had a HeartGram from Ophelia and a message from Holy Hearts. The subject of the latter — Fundraising Details — made dread pool in his stomach, so he opened the one from Ophelia instead. He couldn't remember when she'd first messaged him, but they'd exchanged a few HeartGrams so far, and he kind of liked her.

Okay, more than kind of, but since he wasn't really looking for a relationship, the whole thing confused him.

Hey there,

> *How's it going? Did you read the info about the auction? You should sign up. The money is going to a worthy cause.*

> *I realized recently that you're the second Rick I've met on here that works with computers. I had to backtrack and go find the other one just to make sure I wasn't accidentally picking up the same guy twice. *chuckle**

> *Anything exciting going on at work?*

Work's decent enough on my end, but I'm struggling with a spiritual question. Why, when we know Jesus is enough, do we continue to seek more? Would love to hear your thoughts.

Maverick could feel himself moving on from his temporary insanity where Lia was concerned. Ruining their friendship to find out if there was anything more to their relationship was an all-around bad idea.

It wouldn't be fair to her, but that was only one reason. The rest were summed up with one word: *selfish.* Her friendship meant too much to him, pure and simple. He wouldn't risk it for some crazy hip-noticing moment.

Hi Ophelia –

Boring week at work, but I can live with that. Nothing blew up, and nobody got fired. Like I said, all good.

A friend signed me up for this auction thing. I'd back out if I could find a graceful way to do so. I'd rather donate money than stand on stage for everyone to gawk at.

There. The cat's out of the bag. I'm not the adventurous type. At least not when the adventure means being the center of attention. I'm more of a backstage guy.

As for your question, wow. You don't ask easy ones, do you? I think we will always long for more until we're in heaven and in perfect communion with Christ. Since that kind of closeness can't happen here on earth — it being a fallen world and all — we crave more. The real question isn't why, but rather how we fulfill the need when it arises. Do we seek fulfillment from man (or woman) or from Christ? Does our desire for something more push us closer to Him or further away?

Would love to hear your thoughts as well.

Back to the auction for a minute. Are you coming? Seems like it's time we met. What do you think?

Until next time.

After he sent the HeartGram, Maverick finally reached over with his mouse and double-clicked the subject to open the email.

Holy Hearts
and
Ferito Technology Hospital
would be honored by your presence
at a gala celebration and fundraiser

Join us for

An Informal Affair
&
Bachelor Auction
(no black ties allowed)

He marked the date on his calendar and closed the message only to find another one from Holy Hearts waiting for him. Knowing Lia would ask him about it the next time he saw her, he clicked the *open* button. What he wouldn't do to get out of this.

Thank you for participating in An Informal Affair & Bachelor Auction. As one of our registered bachelors, we want to reassure you that we mean what we say. The auction will be an informal affair. Not only are black ties not required, they're strictly forbidden. In fact, the auction uniform is swimwear. Within the guidelines listed below (including modesty!) we're asking all our bachelors to show up in their swim trunks. We'd like to have a bit of fun with this event. We look forward to seeing you there!

What!? Swim trunks?

Maverick glanced down at his khaki-clad legs. In swim trunks, he'd blind half the people in the audience. Not that he never wore shorts or spent time outside, but they were barely out of winter! Unless they'd all booked time in a tanning booth, every man in attendance should have pasty white legs.

Great.

He'd already invited Ophelia, and something in his gut told him this meeting was important.

What kind of first impression would he make in swim trunks? All kinds of answers flooded Maverick's mind, and none of them were of the positive variety.

Maybe Watts would have an idea. She was a girl, wasn't she? He shot a quick text off to her.

> *Meeting a woman at dreaded bachelor auction and just got news that all the men have to be in swimwear. Help! Need ideas so I don't embarrass myself or blind people.*

There was no immediate reply. The clock on his phone advised him of the late hour. Watts should be…

Ugh. How could he forget?

His baby sister had texted him earlier in the day, excited about her first high altitude night jump, and he'd forgotten about it.

He loved Watts, and he knew she was born to be a paratrooper, but the idea of her jumping out of airplanes still gave him the heebie-jeebies.

Please keep her safe, God. As much as that girl tries to get into trouble, You're the only one strong enough to protect her from herself.

Maverick snapped his laptop closed. It was time for sleep.

141

"I might have met someone."

Maverick glanced up at Lia as she slid into the booth across from him. "Oh?"

Traitor that it was, his heart beat a little faster. He wasn't allowed to be jealous. He'd decided not to pursue Lia, which meant he didn't have the right to be upset about her seeing someone else.

"We're supposed to meet at the auction."

Maverick nodded. "Public place. That's good."

"I always do public places. You know that."

He pushed the menu toward her. "Safety first. Now, do I get a name?"

"Rick."

"What happened to Rod? Y'all's date went well, right?"

Color stained her cheeks. "Um… No spark, I guess. Nothing bad went down."

"So tell me about this Rick guy, then. You guys have been messaging for a while, right?"

"I guess it depends on what you think of as 'a while,' but yeah. He's great. Stable job, sense of humor, and a solid walk with God."

Maverick rearranged his silverware. "Sounds like a winner."

142

"We'll see. I'm almost afraid to get my hopes up, but I like him."

"Hm." He should tell her he'd met someone too, but the words wouldn't come.

"And I was thinking."

He watched her over the top of the menu he was only pretending to read. "Oh?"

"Maybe next week we can eat lunch at that Mexican place by the church."

Well, blow him up, stick a needle in him, and watch him fly away. "Near church?"

Her gaze flicked to his face and back to her menu. "Yeah. I need to let some of my hang-ups go. We're friends. We eat lunch. Trying to hide that from everyone doesn't make sense. Frankly, I'm surprised you've humored me about it for as long as you have."

There was no good way to answer. Humoring her made him condescending. If he argued that he hadn't been humoring her, he was a cad who didn't want to be seen with her.

Maverick did what any sane man would do. He waved the waitress down.

"Let me guess. Double bacon cheeseburger with fries, extra bacon on the side." The waitress stared at him, one eyebrow raised.

"Am I that predictable?"

"Hon, the two of you have been coming here for a year at least. The only thing you've ever changed about your order is when you started adding the extra

143

bacon and that short-lived phase where you decided to drink tea for a while."

"Can I help it that I know what I like?"

The waitress ignored his question and shifted her attention to Lia. "For you?"

"The meatloaf, please, with steamed vegetables."

The waitress glanced back at Maverick. "See? At least she likes to try something new now and then."

Women must be genetically predisposed to band together against men. The waitress could have mentioned the ten month stretch when Lia had eaten nothing but salads, but no. That would have meant siding with Maverick in some weird, twisted way.

He reached for his water and took a long drink.

"I think you might like him."

Maverick stared across the table again. "Who?"

"The guy I met. The one who's coming to the auction. I think you'd like him."

"Oh?"

She shook her head. "Did you forget how to use your words? It's good to talk in sentences. In fact, some women even prefer that."

He extended his hand toward the sweetener packets. Since when was he the fidgeter? "Lay it on me. Why do you think I'd like him?"

"He does something computery." Her nod was decisive.

"Lots of people do computery things. Can you be any more specific?"

"Um. He works for a private employer."

"Oh, that helps."

"It does?" Her eyebrows lifted.

Maverick nodded. "He's one of the millions of people in America who works with computers and isn't employed by the DOD. Piece of cake."

Lia rolled her eyes. "No need to make fun of me."

He reached across the table and gave her folded hands a light nudge. "I'm just teasing. Asking you to describe technology is like asking Watts to explain football. Sometimes it's too funny not to try."

She stole the sweetener packets from him and started sorting them herself. "Have you decided what to wear to the bachelor auction?"

"Did you have to remind me? Swim suits. That was your idea, wasn't it? All because I said women should be auctioned off too. Making it a swimsuit auction is your way of getting back at me. I invited someone to meet me there. Then I saw the message about swimsuits."

A quiet laugh escaped her. "That wasn't me, I promise. It sure is funny, though. Besides, who cares? She'll adore you. So what's her name?"

His eyebrows lifted.

"Can't blame a girl for trying."

"I'll tell you after I've met her. I think you'll like her."

"Just make sure she doesn't have a shellfish allergy before you take her out for seafood."

Maverick shook his head. "Already covered. No known allergies. But thanks for having my back."

Lia chuckled. "Have you decided what to wear?"

"Watts is coming home that weekend. She said she'd help me. Has some brilliant idea or something."

"Um. Is that wise? We're talking about the girl who dyed her hair camouflage for her senior prom."

Maverick leaned his head back against the seat. "I'd forgotten that. This is going to be bad, so very bad."

"Maybe not. I mean, she could…"

He lifted one of his eyebrows and stared at Lia.

She sighed. "I can't lie. This has disaster written all over it. A backup plan might be in order."

"And hurt my sister's feelings? I'd rather walk out on stage and embarrass myself in front of five hundred strangers than disappoint her. She's trained in hand-to-hand combat. I'm pretty sure she can take me down and have me unconscious in two-point-five seconds."

"You're a good brother, you know that? Watts is blessed to have you."

"I'm the one who's blessed. Ferris and I would have grown up to be perfectly ordinary people if it wasn't for her. Can you imagine anything more boring?"

FTEEN

Friday was always a busy day in the ER, but today seemed to be even busier than usual.

Lia walked into cubicle 9A and came to a sudden stop. "What are you doing here?"

"Long story." Agent Whitehall grimaced at her.

"What? Did you ask someone the wrong question?"

"Me? I'm the picture of tact and gentility." He rolled his left shoulder, and his lips thinned.

"How'd you hurt yourself?"

"Hit and run. A woman was trapped in her car with a baby in the back seat, and I smelled gas. I had to get her out."

Lia glanced down at her tablet and saw the police notes in his file. They matched the tale he told. "So you manhandled the door?"

His lips twisted in a half-hearted scowl. "Something like that."

"That's probably easier in a DC walkup with a cheap wood door than on the Beltway with cars made of steel and chrome."

He smirked. "I'm pretty sure this car was more fiberglass than steel."

She extended his left arm and rested one of her hands on top of his shoulder as she moved the wounded arm to test its range of motion. "Did you get the woman and her baby to safety?"

Agent Whitehall nodded. "She and the baby are fine. The gas leak ended up being small, and the car never caught fire. Could have saved myself all this trouble if I'd known that."

"Sure. And stand by while a woman and baby are breathing in gas fumes."

He shrugged his uninjured shoulder. "You've got me there."

Lia continued to rotate his arm into different positions. "Can I ask you a question?"

"Shoot."

"You're Secret Service, right?"

"Last time I checked."

"Did they ever catch the person who shot President Taylor? You know, back before he was president."

Agent Whitehall stiffened and looked like he'd taken a swig of ipecac. "Not yet. Why do you ask?"

She released his arm and began tapping information into her tablet. "When I realized Secret Service was interested in the network security issue, it got me to thinking. What would Secret Service care about our hospital? Then I remembered that President Taylor was treated here after his shooting. We've cared for a couple of vice presidents here, but… It just seemed like it might have something to do with President Taylor. He wasn't president yet back then, but whatever is going on has to be important for Secret Service to be involved."

She glanced up from her tablet when he didn't say anything. He was rubbing his shoulder. Or avoiding eye contact if her inner conspiracy theorist was to be believed.

"Am I crazy?"

He finally made eye contact and gave her a wink. "Now, if I knew something — which I'm not saying I do — it'd be illegal for me to tell you. In fact, it'd be illegal for me to tell you I don't know anything, either. National security and all that. As for you being crazy… maybe you should check with a doctor about that one. I'm not qualified to say…"

"Your interpersonal skills could use a little work."

"You wound me. I'm as charming as the day is long."

"What, on the winter solstice? The shortest day of the year?"

Agent Whitehall's bark of laughter filled the cubicle. "So can I go home now, or what?"

Lia shook her head. "It doesn't feel like anything's broken or torn, but this was only a cursory exam. My suggestion is ice and acetaminophen. Talk to your primary care physician about getting an x-ray if it's still causing you discomfort in forty-eight hours."

"Can't you x-ray it now?"

"I'm not in the habit of ordering tests I think are unnecessary."

"As long as you can clear me for work without the x-ray."

"Oh…" She glanced from her tablet back up to the agent. "I still recommend forty-eight hours off."

"Not gonna happen." His voice was commanding and his headshake decisive, but the hint of a smile that touched his lips softened the response.

She sighed. "Fine. Let me see if I can find an open spot in the radiology schedule."

A few taps on the tablet later, and Lia peeked up at Agent Whitehall. "You're in luck. They have an opening in the Mammography Department."

"The what?"

"The mammography department. Where women get mammograms."

Agent Whitehall glanced down at the front of his shirt. "Um..."

Lia shook her head. "Sorry. The Radiology Department is laid out weird. Most x-rays are taken care of on the east side, but there's one small x-ray room on the west side. That's where I found an opening. You have to go to the Mammography

Department to reach it, though. I'll go print your paperwork out, and have you on your way."

She left the cubicle and headed for the printer. He was required to check in for his x-ray at Mammography's front desk. Should she tell him that or let him figure it out on his own?

She hadn't yet decided when Dr. Zagel's voice rang from across the bullpen. "Code Gusher in 2B! Code Gusher! All hands on deck!"

Oh, boy. The hospital administration had warned him not to use that one. She jogged back to Agent Whitehall, handed the paperwork off to him. "Susie at the front desk will tell you where to go. You'll have to wait around for someone to read your results, but Radiology can give you a work release. Even with the federal code on the request, it'll take a while. You might want to stop in the gift shop and get a book."

Then she was out of his room and heading for 2B at top speed. She arrived in time to hear a string of curses fly from the doctor's mouth. She moved the curtain aside and stepped into the cubicle. She didn't ask. The scene told the story.

Heaps of bloody bandages littered the floor, Dr. Zagel's face was a thundercloud of anger, and two nurses crowded close to the body, one squeezing air into the patient's lungs with the Ambu bag and the other providing chest compressions. They couldn't stop until the doctor called time of death.

"Dr. Zagel." He ignored her, and Lia tried again, louder. "Dr. Zagel.

He closed his eyes and took a deep breath before glancing at his watch. "Time of death, 4:35pm."

The two nurses stepped away from the body. Lia would say something to them, but not right now. They all still had patients in other cubicles who needed their help. Lia pivoted in the small space, ready to go. That's when she noticed her shoes. Blood had pooled on the bed and run off the edge, dripping down onto her left foot and coating the shoe.

She would have rather ended up with vomit on them than a dead man's blood. Vomit was easier to wash off… and to forget.

Lia trudged toward the parking garage.

There was something about watching a man's lifeblood drain away that made a person think. She kept getting hung up on small things. In the whole big scheme of life, how she looked didn't really matter. There were so many things that were life or death, but what she saw in the mirror wasn't one of them. Neither was her dating life.

Peace rolled through her in waves. She was loved by the One who mattered. He loved her when she was full of energy and when she was bone tired. He loved her when her life was orderly and when she was a mess. He loved her when she ate a greasy burger and when she ate a dressingless salad. He loved her even on those days that she had a hard time loving herself.

Thank you, God.

She wouldn't lie to herself and say the battle was over, but she could take a second to thank God for the insight He'd given her.

"Hey."

Lia's head lifted, and all the weighty thoughts she'd been mulling slipped away. "Maverick. What are you doing here?"

"I heard about a death in the ER. I didn't know if it was one of yours or not, but I thought maybe you could use a friend."

"Not mine, but I was there."

"Do you want to catch some dinner and talk?"

She shook her head. "I'm tired. I need to get home while I'm still alert enough to drive."

"Okay. Can I at least give you a hug first?" The dim lighting of the parking garage turned his hair midnight dark while it stole the color from his eyes and replaced it with shadow, but he was still the same Maverick. A friend. Someone she could rely on.

"Sure. I could go for one of those."

155

He enfolded her in his arms and pulled her close. "I'm sure you did everything in your power."

Lia rested her head against his chest and wrapped her arms around his waist. She was ready to fall asleep where she stood. Maverick made her heart lighter, always had. Like everything would work out. He was a good friend, and standing in the circle of his embrace was the closest she'd come to a successful date in months.

He withdrew his arms and tucked his hands into his pockets, putting an end to their sort-of hug. "Are you ready for tomorrow's informal, non-black-tie gala affair?"

She missed his touch, but that didn't make sense. This was Maverick. A hug from him had never felt weird before, so why were her insides turning to jelly?

"Earth to Lia."

She took a deep breath and tried to push away the quivering that had taken up residence in her middle. "I will be after I take a shower and get some sleep. Did you sort out your swimsuit situation?"

"Watts arrives early afternoon, and she's refused to tell me what she found for me to wear."

"Oh dear."

"Exactly. She's bringing Wesley with her, too."

"Not for me, I hope."

Maverick shook his head. "Seems they're dating now. Ferris has already gone through the folks' house and removed most of the pictures mom had on the walls."

Huh? "Why…?"

"When Watts was in the seventh grade, Johnny Baker said he didn't want to go to the dance with her because her hair was too short. She cried. That's when Ferris started collecting dead animals."

"Dead…? You're kind of creeping me out."

"He bought them wherever he found them. Yard sales, estate sales, you name it. They're all stuffed, not just dead. I probably should have said that part first."

"Um…" What could she say to that? "Ferris has always had a unique sense of humor."

"Unique. Ha. Nice one." Maverick scratched his chin. "He's transformed Mom and Dad's house into a taxidermist's paradise. And a sister's boyfriend's nightmare."

"Oh, dear." The woman who fell in love with Ferris someday would need to be special. A bizarre sense of humor wouldn't hurt either. "I can't believe your folks are letting him."

"They've sort of been out of town for the last two days. They should arrive home around the time that Watts and Wesley roll in."

Lia covered her eyes. "Oh dear, dear, dear, dear, dear."

157

"I hid a video camera so we can catch everyone's expressions as they come in the front door."

Lia chuckled. "You'd better retrieve your swim costume from Watts before she steps over that threshold because if she sees what you let Ferris do first, she may torch whatever she brought."

"I'm not convinced that would be a bad thing." Maverick took the keys from her hand and unlocked the car door for her. "Your chariot awaits, m'lady. Text me when you get home so I know you made it safely, 'kay?"

"Will do."

Maverick closed the door and stood there as she drove away.

Lia arrived home, but the urge to crawl into bed had abandoned her. What was a girl to do when she was home alone and not ready for sleep?

She sent Maverick a "made it" text before flipping the TV on and finding one of her favorite police procedurals. Then she reached for her laptop and booted it up.

A HeartGram from Rick awaited her.

Looking forward to seeing you. As requested, I'll be wearing a pink shirt. I sure hope that's your sense of humor showing through and not some crazy obsession with pink-clad men. If you ask for pink pants next, we might need to talk.

Hope you had a good day at work. Since I don't know what you do, I'm not sure if that means an uneventful one or a busy one. It should be fun to fill in the blanks once we meet.

In the meantime, I should go try on my swim trunks and goggles.

See you soon.

Lia hit the reply button and started typing.

You're such a hoot. Yes, I am a pink-obsessed crazy. I buy everyone pink socks for Christmas and only date men who wear pink underwear.

She looked at that last part. Funny, but too suggestive. She backspaced.

...and only date men who drive pink cars, although mopeds are also acceptable.

I've enjoyed this chance to get acquainted with you without all the day-to-day stuff imposing. It's added a bit of mystery to the whole thing.

So tomorrow I'll be looking for the mysterious man in the pink shirt.

159

She'd been so fed up with men in general when Rick had first reached out to her that she'd suggested guidelines. No specifics about jobs or family. He'd agreed, so he must not have found her request too bizarre.

They'd spent over a month exchanging messages almost every day. She knew about his heart for God, his sense of humor, and a few quirky things like how many words per minute he could type and how nervous he'd been when he left home for college.

Lia would have laughed if a character in a movie had said that, but she felt like she knew him on a deeper level. There was something good and wholesome in him. She couldn't help but feel like God was nudging her in his direction.

Why, then, as she finally climbed into bed and drifted off to sleep, were her thoughts all about Maverick and that hug he'd given her? Why was Maverick's cologne suddenly so sexy if God wanted her to date Rick? *Did* God want her to date Rick, or had she just assumed that?

Sixteen

Maverick watched her drive away.

What was he doing? He was supposed to be over the temporary insanity. But then he'd put his arms around Lia, drawing her close. He'd only wanted to comfort her, but the smell of her shampoo had filled his head. Was it his fault she fit perfectly against his chest?

He'd stuck his hands in his pockets as soon as he'd let her go to stop himself from reaching out and pulling her back.

Ophelia would be at the auction tomorrow night. He liked her. A lot. It wasn't fair to string her along if he continued to carry some crazy blazing torch for another woman.

What a mess.

His phone rang as he sauntered back to his own car, but he didn't recognize the incoming number. "Hello?"

"Mr. Hoyt?"

"Yes."

"Butch here. Butch Hutchinson."

Huh. The cybersecurity team had left a week ago, but nobody had ever said a word about whether or not they'd figured out who was behind the hack. "What can I do for you?"

"The IT department at the hospital there will be undergoing some changes over the next few weeks. I thought I owed it to you to tell you in person. Or over the phone as the case may be."

I owed it to you to tell you in person.

He'd thought Mr. Planter would be the one firing him. He hadn't expected it to come from Hutchinson.

"…a week or two to get up to speed, but I believe you're up to the task."

Maverick must have zoned out, because he had no idea what Hutchinson was talking about. "What?"

A loud sigh came over the line. "Mr. Planter has been let go. You've been promoted. On Monday when you report to work, you will be in charge of the IT department."

"I just left for the day, and Mr. Planter was still running things."

"Be that as it may, this is a done deal. Mr. Planter was terminated at the end of the work day. You will take over on Monday. I expect you to make the transition as smooth as possible for the other IT staff and for the rest of the hospital. My idea of a smooth transition is that nobody outside the IT department even realizes there's been a change. Are you ready for the challenge?"

"I… Yes. Yes I am."

"Good. Any questions?"

Dozens, but he'd start small. "Was Mr. Planter involved with the network problems?"

"No. Nobody at the hospital had anything to do with it. It was an outside attack. However, Mr. Planter's choice to risk hospital security so he could protect his job is unacceptable. He would have allowed a serious security breach to continue unreported and unrepaired, and that's not how we do business at Ferito Technology."

"Of course. Have you caught the culprits?"

"No. We repaired the breach and installed stronger security measures, but the person behind it has eluded us. Now, as long as you have no other questions, I'll let you go."

So this was what it felt like to be picked up and thrown into the deep end… if the deep end was full of hungry piranhas. "Who do I turn to when I have technical questions?"

"You troubleshoot and try to find the answer. Failing that, you call me on this number, and I'll make sure you get whatever assistance you need. With one exception. Anytime there is any kind of security threat, you call me immediately, no questions asked."

"Understood."

"Very well then."

Butch Hutchinson was going to hang up, and this conversation would be over. Employee Maverick might have been able to let that happen, but supervisor Maverick couldn't. "Wait!"

"Yes, Mr. Hoyt?"

"Um. Whitehall. Why… Should I be concerned about the Secret Service's presence at the hospital?"

Silence filled the line for a few more heartbeats than Maverick was comfortable with before a reply came. "Agent Whitehall was brought in to consult on a matter, and I took advantage of that presence to have him vet you. He spoke to your co-workers and some of the medical personnel you deal with the most. Because of the hospital's proximity to DC, it seemed a reasonable precaution to take. In any event, you passed. If you run into him again, it'll either be a coincidence or a serious problem. I trust you to be capable of telling the difference."

"Of course. Thank you Mr. Hutchinson."

"Do the job and do it well. That's all the thanks I require."

The phone clicked into silence before Maverick could respond.

He still didn't know who was behind the cyber-attack on the hospital's network. He'd have to ask the next time he had reason to speak with Butch Hutchinson. Until then, he would be content with the biggest promotion of his career. A celebration was in order.

Lia was on her way home and not in the mood. With his folks out of town and Watts off doing her thing, that left only Ferris. Maverick's fingers flashed across the screen of this phone until he got to Ferris' name. "Hey little brother, you're coming out to dinner with me. My treat."

"Why?"

"Do I need a reason?"

"No. You can buy me a meal anytime, but if this is some lame attempt to get me out of the house so someone can sneak in and remove all the animals from the walls, I'm gonna have to fight you."

"I got some good news and wanted to celebrate. No ulterior motive. Keep asking me questions, though, and I'll rescind the offer."

"No questions here. Where are we meeting, and how much time do I have? I've been trying to mount my buffalo head up above the doorway."

"Isn't that one fake?"

"Yeah. It's plastic. But if I mount it high enough, he won't be able to tell."

"He saw the house the last time he came down with Watts. Remember? He's going to notice the difference."

"All the better. He'll notice the difference, and he'll know why. Point made."

Maverick shook his head. "The buffalo's overkill. Meet me at the diner on Fifteenth and Broadville in about twenty minutes."

"That should give me enough time to roll the Howitzer into the living room. See you in twenty-five!"

For the second time that night, the line was dead before Maverick could speak. A Howitzer? Where on earth had Ferris found a Howitzer? Then again…

He was better off not knowing.

Maverick put his car in reverse and pulled out of the parking spot. His family… Never a dull moment, not even when he wanted one.

Seventeen

Lia woke to sunshine and blue skies. It was going to be an exceptional day. The bachelor auction would be a magnificent success, not to mention fun.

Fun in an irreverent sort of way. The men would all be good sports. How could they not? After all, they were going to be on stage. They kind of had to play along.

Lia had volunteered to help, but as it turned out, Jezriel didn't seem to need her. The woman from Holy Hearts had planned the event faster than most people sang the National Anthem. She still wanted Lia there early, though, just in case something came up.

As far as Lia was concerned, her biggest contribution had been signing Maverick up to be auctioned off.

Couples all across the country were being encouraged to come meet each other for the first time at one of these Holy Hearts fundraising events. A lot of the men going up on the auction block were hospital employees, but almost as many were Holy Hearts clients hoping to encounter their special someone.

Including Rick.

Lia let out the adult version of a dreamy sigh as she searched her closet for the perfect outfit.

If only…

Lia shook her head.

She'd had a bad day yesterday, and Maverick had given her a friendly hug… that hadn't *felt* friendly. Lia didn't even know what more-than-friendly should feel like, but she knew the zinging of her nerves last night hadn't been friendly-hug-from-guy-she'd-known-her-whole-life zings. What was she supposed to think of that?

Trying to be something more than friends with Maverick would be a disaster. Their lousy track records spoke volumes, and a relationship that ended badly would also ruin their friendship.

Their future had been set since the fourth grade. That was when Lia had decided they would grow up, get married to other people, and raise their kids together. Her daughter would marry his son — or vice versa — and they'd become grandparents jointly in their golden years.

It was a reasonable, solid plan.

And Rick was a fantastic guy.

Why, then, had standing in the circle of Maverick's arms last night left her wishing Rick would stand her up?

Could it be a fever? That might explain it.

Lia felt her forehead, but it was cool to the touch. No help there.

168

Am I losing my mind, God? I'm pretty sure Maverick's off limits, so if you could quell all these weird feelings about him, that would be handy.

Lia yanked a deep purple wraparound dress out of her closet. It was elegant without being so over-the-top that she'd stand out in a crowd that had hopefully followed the instructions to leave their black tie attire at home.

After tucking the dress and a few cosmetics into her garment bag, Lia was armed for the first part of the day.

Several hours later, Lia stood behind a curtain on stage left and peeked out at the assembled crowd. The hotel's wait staff served the meal, but instead of their usual black and white uniforms, they wore black pants and Hawaiian shirts.

Many of the people in attendance had gone for the dressy casual look. One table in the back, however, was full of women in swim suits who acted like they might have spent some time in the hotel bar before making their way into the ballroom. They looked like they were ready to bid and bid high.

Rick had said he would be there, but his name wasn't on the list of men being auctioned off. No

Rick, Richard, or any other derivation. Maybe he was in the audience instead. Her eyes roamed the crowd, but she found no pink shirts out there among the sea of people.

"Chop, chop, everyone. Places!" Jezriel clapped her hands, and the men backstage began to fall into line.

The first man up for auction wore swim trunks that covered him to his knees and a ribbed tank top that showed off his deltoids.

"Ladies and Gentlemen, let me introduce you to our first bachelor of the evening. His name's Hank, and he likes taking long walks on the beach and buying chocolate for the women in his life. We'll start the bidding at $25."

Within minutes, Hank was auctioned off to the healthy tune of $125. The first ten bachelors all went in quick succession. When Lia got a look at the next bachelor, though, she did a double-take. "Dr. Zagel?"

He glanced over at her and frowned. "It's for a good cause."

"I know. I just didn't expect to bump into you here. You're not usually…" Approachable? Kind? Compassionate? Human?

Jezriel called the doctor to the stage, and he disappeared before Lia could think of a fitting word to complete her sentence.

"Next up, Dr. Malachi Zagel. He's used to the fast pace of the ER, and he's looking for someone who can keep up with him as he goes through life at a hundred miles an hour. Oh, and he paid his way through med school by working as a masseuse, ladies. And that was before he joined the Army. What do you think ladies? A doctor with magic fingers and a military bod."

Dr. Zagel, in black sunglasses, faded blue swim trunks, and his physician's coat, struck several comic body-building poses as the bidding became more and more heated.

"I have $300 from the lady in pink. $350 from the woman in the back. $400 from the grandma at the front table. $500 back to the lady in pink. $750 from the woman in the back. $1000 from the grandma up front here. Going once, going twice… Sold for $1000!"

Lia peeked out at Dr. Z's winning bidder. She had to be seventy if she was a day.

She glanced back at the line of men waiting to be auctioned off and saw… *Oh goodness gracious sakes alive.*

There stood Maverick. He wore black trunks that almost reached his knees, hot pink flippers on his feet, a hot pink men's swim shirt, a face mask and snorkel with a thick smear of neon green sunblock on his nose. And a giant inflatable duck around his middle.

171

What, oh what, had Watts done to that poor man?

Lia rushed over to him. "Are you sure about this? You can change. I'm sure Watts will understand."

He shook his head. "I promised her I'd wear the entire outfit."

"Before or after you saw it?"

"Before."

"Some promises are okay to break."

"She kind of threatened to rat me out about something if I didn't do as she said."

Lia gave Maverick's shoulder a light shove. "She's your sister. She's been threatening to rat you out since the age of two. You won't get grounded if you stand up to her once in a while."

Maverick bit his bottom lip and gave his head the slightest shake. "Not this time." Then he tapped his cheek. "A kiss for luck?"

Lia stretched up on her toes and brushed her lips against Maverick's cheek. "It's not too late."

He gave her a sad smile and moved a step closer to the curtain as the emcee summoned another bachelor out to the stage. "Yeah, it kind of is." He tipped his head toward to the corner where she'd been standing. "Go, enjoy the rest of the auction and have a wonderful time with your mystery man today."

"I don't think he came."

"Why not? I thought you guys hit it off."

172

"We have been. We are. But I haven't seen him yet. I don't think he's out there."

"Is he one of the bachelors?"

"No. He's not on the list. It's okay, though. We were going to meet in the lobby after the event."

Maverick gave her another smile that didn't quite reach his eyes. "Must be the plan for a lot of people. You're the seventh person so far that's told me that's where they planned to meet their Holy Hearts counterpart today." He tweaked the end of her nose. "Don't give up. Even if this guy is dumb enough not to show up, God's not going to hang you out to dry. You won't be alone."

"I know." Lia nodded. "God and I are okay. If this one doesn't pan out, I'm done. I finally figured out that in Christ, I am enough. I'm complete already. I don't need a man — or anything else — to make me that way."

"I'm glad. I'd hug you, but I'm afraid the duck here might make that more awkward then it needs to be."

Lia shook her head. "When you're ready to plot your payback against Watts, let me know. I want in on it."

IGHTEEN

Maverick watched Lia walk back to her observation corner as a round of catcalls erupted from the audience out front. Somebody would be fetching a high price today.

He glanced down at the duck around his waist. Someone would take pity on him and not leave him standing on stage without any bids. Surely at least one woman out there could claim a sense of humor like his sister's. He hoped.

"Please welcome our next bachelor, Maverick Hoyt!"

He tried to take a deep breath, but his lungs didn't want to work properly. Maverick stepped out through the curtain and prayed he wouldn't complete the picture by passing out.

"Maverick is a certified computer geek who…" The woman's voice faded away, and Maverick was left with no choice but to open his eyes.

Every person in the ballroom stared at him.

The woman with the microphone broke the spell. "Oh ladies, you have to bid on this one! After you've worked a long day, or the kids have been whining since two in the morning, this is what you need. A man who is willing to go to any lengths to make you laugh. Life will never be boring with a guy like this. I'm going to start the bidding at $100."

Say what?

Just like that, paddles started raising all over the place. The bidding reached $500, and Maverick managed to force his lungs into submission. He sucked in a big breath of life-giving air while trying to prevent his jaw from hitting the stage floor.

"I have $900 from the swimsuit table back there and $1000 from the blonde in fatigues."

Oh, thank goodness. Maverick's eyes roamed the ballroom until he found her. Watts was bidding on him.

"$1200 back to the swimsuit table. Going once... Now we have $1500 from the woman in black. $1700 at the swimsuit table. $1800 to the blonde in fatigues. And $2000 from the lady in black."

Watts put down her paddle. Great. She must be out of money. If he could send her a telepathic message telling her to keep bidding, he would.

"Going once, going twice..."

"$2500!"

Maverick's head whipped around to find the source of the voice. There, standing off to the far side, barely visible because of the stage's shape. Lia to the rescue. Sweet Lia.

The woman with the microphone — what was her name again? — nodded in Lia's direction.

"Going once, going twice…sold for $2500! Or, rented at least."

Maverick's heart slammed inside his chest. How could one man be so cotton-pickin' mixed up?

He was supposed to meet Ophelia today, and he'd been looking forward to that moment for weeks.

Then Lia had stepped out from behind the stage and paid premium dollar for him, and his heart acted like it was so much more than just a friendly gesture.

He shouldn't have hugged her last night. He'd obviously taken leave of his senses.

Premium dollar…

Her car fund. She'd spent the money intended to replace her on-death's-door car.

Now he felt like an even worse heel.

He was here to meet one woman, and his heart was short-circuiting over someone else.

Cad.

Scoundrel.

Worm.

Head down, Maverick made his way past the remaining to-be-auctioned men. His first order of business — get to the dressing room. Next, straighten out this whole thing. He needed to pick one and be done with it. He was never meant to be the man who couldn't decide between two women. As a self-proclaimed computer geek, he'd always known he would be lucky if he ever got one woman to look at him seriously. But two? That was one too many.

He yanked his duffel bag from the corner where he'd stashed it and began pulling out clothes. At least he could get rid of the duck before he met Ophelia. Wearing real pants would be a step up, too. It would be nice if, as soon as he saw her, he knew what to do.

God, wisdom please. It's not supposed to be like this.

Maybe it was time to swear off all relationships.

The heavy knot in Maverick's stomach tightened. He refused to tell Lia about his feelings and risk losing her friendship, but he couldn't date Ophelia when his heart hurt over another woman.

Yep. Time to swear off women altogether. Definitely.

Maverick caught sight of his scowl in the mirror. Hm. He didn't appear to be as crazy about that idea as he wanted to be.

Tension squeezed his chest, but he knew what to do. He didn't like it, but the alternatives were all unthinkable. He needed to be able to live with himself at the end of the day.

NINETEEN

Lia sat in a corner of the lobby. She pulled the faux diamond headband out of her hair as she watched yet another couple pair off. Pink-shirted Rick was a no-show.

She closed her eyes and rubbed at the ball of stress in the middle of her forehead.

Agreeing to meet Rick had been a mistake. She should have listened to Maverick when he'd balked about signing up for Holy Hearts.

Instead, she was scheduled to make that all-important face-to-face connection with a man she'd only just started getting to know and like. Then last night she'd gone and leaned her head against the chest of her best friend, and the whole world had turned inside out and upside down.

Maverick would meet his mystery woman today, and Lia couldn't intrude on that. She might be wrapped up in her own misery, but she didn't want to ruin his special day in the process.

Maverick. Funny, funny Maverick.

Lia's hand fisted around her headband, the stones cutting into her palm. She glanced down at it before staring vacantly across the lobby. Rick had asked her to wear a tiara, but when she'd searched for something graceful and elegant, all she'd found were big garish displays of cut glass. The headband suited her better. It was subtle, but if he really wanted to meet her, he'd find her.

Only, he hadn't. Somewhere during her musings, the lobby had emptied out, and she was now alone.

So be it.

Lia stood, put the jeweled elastic headband back in its place, straightened her spine, and headed to the wide glass doors leading out to the hotel's portico. Her hand was on the vertical brass handle of the door when the doorman opened it from the other side. She nodded to him and began to step through the marble entryway.

"Lia?"

She froze at the sound of the familiar voice. Great. Maverick wanted to introduce her to his mystery woman.

A broad smile plastered into place, Lia circled back toward the lobby.

A firing squad would be more fun than this.

She re-crossed the threshold back into the hotel before making eye contact with the conspicuously alone Maverick. "Where's your date?"

His head tilted infinitesimally to the right as he stared at her. "I'm still working on that. What about your date? Rick, isn't it?"

She shrugged and fought to keep her faux smile in place. "Guess he didn't liked what he saw. At least this way I don't get stuck with the bill."

"Speaking of… Thank you for saving me from the barracuda in the back. You're going to let me repay you, aren't you? Your car fund…"

She waved away his offer. "You'd have done the same for me."

Maverick tapped a finger to the side of his head. "I like your headband. You weren't wearing it backstage earlier. Was that for Rick?"

Lia tugged at the elastic and resisted the urge to yank it off and shove it in her purse. "He wanted a tiara, but this was the best I could do."

"Tiara, huh? Sounds like he wanted you to feel like a princess."

She snorted. "That only works if the prince shows up."

Maverick's gaze darted to her headband before returning to her face. "You've been seeing this Rick guy online for months. You first mentioned him not too long after…um…the one who cleaned his ears with a fork."

"There was a Rick back then. It didn't work out. He met someone else and got engaged before we ever had a chance. This is a new one. Guess I should scratch that name off my list. No more Ricks for me."

Lia started to pull the headband from her hair when Maverick reached out and stilled her arm. "Leave it. You make it look good."

She dropped her hand to her side. "You're acting weird, Mav. What's up?"

"I told you I hid my picture...?"

She nodded but didn't speak. Maverick used to tell her that getting answers from her was harder than shelling pecans with bare hands. Why break tradition now?

"When did you hide yours?"

"After I... I decided to focus on meeting people who liked me for me, not for what I look like. If the people talking to me online were preoccupied with my appearance, then how could I leave that in my past? I wanted to be a healthier me – not so concerned about weight and stuff – so it made sense to block my picture."

"And to date men who had theirs blocked, too?"

"Well, yeah. It was only fair."

He tilted his head to the side. "You marked your profile as friends-only."

She gave a slight nod. "That same day."

"I've known you practically my whole life." Maverick took a step back and inspected her.

A flush climbed Lia's neck at the attention.

"All this time, and I never knew Lia was short for something else."

"Now how on earth did you…" Her gaze snapped to his face. The light in his blue eyes flashed, and the world tilted on its axis. He wasn't pushing her buttons or teasing her. So then, what…? "Maverick…?"

"My name's on the distinctive side, in case you haven't noticed."

Lia nodded, hope fluttering in her chest.

"I signed up for Holy Hearts using a nickname."

"Your nickname is Mav."

"Well, sure, but that's obvious too. I didn't want people I worked with to be able to go online and find my dating profile."

"You work with a bunch of men in the IT Department. Nobody would go looking for your profile."

He shrugged. "It made sense at the time."

The wings of hope beat faster. "So what nickname did you come up with?"

The corner of his mouth tipped up. "How did I never know your name is Ophelia?"

She resisted the urge to stomp her foot. "You're not wearing a pink shirt. You have some explaining to do."

Maverick threw back his head and laughed. "Did you not see me up there on that stage? That shirt couldn't have gotten any pinker."

Her laughter bubbled up. "She must have shopped a long time to find something so blinding." Then she took a step closer to him. "You were supposed to wear a pink shirt here, in the lobby, to meet me. But…" She poked his chest. "You're wearing black. What gives?"

He captured her hand in his own and held it to his chest. "I couldn't do it. I couldn't go on a date with Ophelia when my heart beats for someone else."

"I'm Ophelia."

His eyes crinkled at the corners. "I didn't know that, now did I? Not when you first messaged me, and not in all the time since. Not until you turned around to face me with diamonds in your hair."

"They're not real diamonds."

"Might as well be. You make them look like a million bucks."

"You're supposed to say I look like a million bucks."

"Stop underestimating yourself. You look way better than that."

Lia rested her other hand against Maverick's black-clad chest. "I planned to dump Rick anyway, the louse."

"You did?"

She kept her eyes trained on the buttons of his shirt. "A friend gave me a hug last night. My best friend in the whole world. And as quick as a flash of lightning, he stopped being my friend."

His eyes widened, and their blue depths shimmered with...something. Joy? Maybe with a touch of laughter. "He did?"

Lia gave a quick nod. "He became a man. A kind-hearted, God-fearing, sexy-as-all-get-out man, who held me after a bad day and who didn't push me to talk about it. He's nearly perfect. That is, if you can ignore his taste in swimwear."

Maverick's chest rumbled under her fingers. "I'll take credit for giving you a hug, but Watts get all the credit for the swimwear."

She glanced up, and her eyes got snagged on his. "What is Watts holding over you? You never told me."

His gaze slid to the side. "Um... She put two-and-two together after her last visit. Figured out how I... She threatened to tell you how I felt if I didn't wear what she brought."

"You didn't want me to know."

TWENTY

Maverick wanted to wrap his arms around Lia and pull her close. This thing budding between them was still delicate, though, and he couldn't face the thought of crushing it. "You had Rick. I couldn't take that away from you. I'm not heartless."

She smoothed her hand over his thudding heart. "Far from it."

"So where do we go from here?" Maverick lifted the hand he still held in his own and brought it to his lips. "I'm not sure I can go back to the way things were before."

"I'm not sure I want to." Lia stared into his eyes as if she was drinking in his very essence, and he didn't mind one bit.

His gaze dropped to her mouth. He didn't want to rush her, but...

"What attracted you to Ophelia, anyway?"

Maverick leaned back on his heels. "Honestly? Her name."

Lia's brow furrowed.

He shrugged. "Ophelia's a unique name, and I figured if things went haywire, I could spin it into an entertaining story. I have this friend, see, and I like to tell her stories that make her laugh."

"You've been sabotaging your dates to give me something to laugh about?"

"Not at first." He ran a hand through his hair. The ground beneath his feet became ocean sand, shifting quicker than he could find his bearings. "At some point, I realized I didn't really care about dating. You did, though, and I couldn't let you go through it alone. I'd already had a couple of bad dates by then, so why not? That was around the time Sven-the-jerk came along and took you skiing."

She winced.

"I couldn't abandon you, so I embraced it. I decided to put our dare to good use."

"What about all the women you dated? Their feelings were on the line."

He shook his head. "I always made it clear. Friends only. Until Ophelia. There was something about her that made me wonder if we could be more. It pulled me in and stopped me from giving her the never-more-than-friends speech before our first meeting."

"I felt that way about Rick, too. I… I had decided friends-only, but he was different. Every HeartGram he sent brought out laughter in me… and brought us closer together."

Lia swayed ever-so-slightly, and Maverick took advantage of it. He leaned in until he felt her breath against his lips. This would be a moment they would both remember for years to come. They would retell this story to their grandchildren someday.

"Kiss her already!"

Maverick whipped his head around to look at their party crasher. "Watts, what are you doing here?"

"You think I came all this way just to bring you swim trunks, bro? I'm not leaving till you seal the deal." With that, Watts crossed her arms and jutted one hip out in that annoying rebellious way she'd developed back in middle school.

Lia chuckled. "No pressure, right?"

Oh for the days when he could throttle his little sister and then pretend Ferris had done it. "I don't think I can do it with Watts watching. Our first kiss should be special."

Lia's hazel eyes darkened for a second. But then she nodded, pulled her hand from his, and took a step back. "That makes sense. I think it's only proper you wine me and dine me first anyway. In fact, now that I think about it, I have a kissing policy. No kissing on the first, second, or third date." She tapped her high-heeled foot on the floor. "Yes, I think that's correct. So I guess you'll have to ask me out."

If Watts were any closer — and if Wesley weren't standing guard — Maverick would be more than half-tempted to go all linebacker on her. Or as linebacker as a computer geek could go.

He took a deep breath, then another. This situation required more than one. "Lia, would you do me the honor of joining me for dinner this evening at six? On a date?"

She tapped her chin. "What do you think, Watts? Do I have plans, or am I available?"

Wesley jumped into the conversation. "Oh, for the love of butterflies and unicorns, get it over with and put us all out of our misery!"

Maverick and Lia both swiveled their heads to look at the young couple. Watts shrugged. "He has five sisters and scads of nieces. You have to make allowances."

With a shake of her head, Lia returned her attention to Maverick and nodded. "Alright. A date. Tonight. Our first date, by my count."

"Don't remind me. I have to wait through three of them before I can even think about kissing you."

Lia turned her back to Maverick so fast that he had to take a step back to keep his balance. She waved across the lobby to where Watts and Wesley stood. "Thank you for the swimwear. You're a good sister."

Wesley snorted. "She figured the only way to force you two together was to cause maximum embarrassment in as public a way as possible."

Maverick pinched the bridge of his nose. He needed to get Lia out of there before either Watts or Wesley said anything else.

Before he formulated a plan, though, Lia spun back toward him. Her balance had to be off, too, because she lurched into him.

He grabbed her close before she completely lost her footing.

Her mouth, mere millimeters from his chin, begged his attention. How mad would she be if he ignored her three date rule?

His decision hadn't yet crystallized when her hazel eyes drifted closed.

He was only human. Surely she'd forgive him for breaking the rules this once.

Maverick stepped through that last tiny bit of distance and kissed the woman he loved, the woman who had been his best friend for more years than he could count, the woman whose hips swayed in the most distracting manner, the woman who held his heart and all his tomorrows in the palm of her hand.

 Twenty- One

Lia's heart sighed.

Then it took off racing in her chest like an out-of-control tambourine.

But she didn't mind one bit.

She sank into Maverick's kiss while she soaked up his love. He hadn't said it yet, but it pulsed there between them.

Love.

It was a living thing, solid and strong. Years of friendship could do that, could give a relationship resilience and surety.

Lia inhaled the scent of Maverick's cologne. Somehow, in the last twenty-four hours, the fragrance he wore had morphed from reasonably masculine to downright sexy. Now, in the light of day, it was even more nuanced. It smelled like tomorrow, like happily-ever-after.

Maverick pulled away before she was ready. "I hope you'll forgive me."

She ran her fingers along his jaw and up the side of his face. "For what?"

"Breaking the three date rule."

Life would be so much fun with this man by her side. "I said no kissing on the first, second, or third date. I didn't say anything about before… or after."

His eyebrows shot up.

"Why do you think I faked a fall?"

Maverick looked from her to the floor where she'd magically tripped over nothing. "You faked it?"

"You were being too much of a gentleman. I figured that was the easiest way to land myself in your arms."

He scratched his head. "That whole wave thing and talking to Watts across the lobby was part of a ploy?"

She nodded, twirled around, and gave a pageant wave to where Watts and Wesley still stood on the other side of the lobby before giving her attention back to Maverick.

Maverick bent his arm and held his elbow out to her, a smile splitting his face.

Lia slipped her hand through the crook of his arm and leaned into his side as he led her toward the hotel's entrance.

As the doorman opened the glass door for them, Maverick angled close and whispered in her ear. "I plan to spend the rest of my life with you."

Lia's heart thrilled at his words. All the bad dates, uncertainty, self-doubt, and yes, even the Network Elf, had all brought her here to this moment. "You should know I don't accept marriage proposals on the first, second, or third date, either."

Maverick examined his watch. "Hm. Looks like it's half past four. That gives me over an hour before we're officially on our first date."

Oh yes. Life promised to be fun with this man, and she couldn't wait for the adventure to begin.

The End

Author's Note

Thank you for taking the time to read *An Informal Affair*. I hope you enjoyed Maverick and Lia's story. I loved writing about them and exploring the fun world of online dating. Contrary to my portrayal of it, online dating isn't *always* a disaster. I have several happily married friends who met via online dating. Thank goodness, right? Because nobody deserves to go through all the bad dates that poor Lia got stuck with!

If you can, please take a minute to tell others about this book by leaving a review on Amazon and Goodreads. I wouldn't mind if you told all your friends about it, too. Or took out an ad in your local paper... although that might get costly. In all seriousness, though, reviews are golden, and I appreciate every single one of them.

As any writer will tell you, gratitude is a way of life in this line of work. I am beyond thankful that God gives me stories to share and the words with which to tell them. He has allowed me to do something I love, and it's a blessing every single day. Writing isn't a solitary journey, though, and I want to thank the people who have helped pull this story together and make it shine.

Thank you to e everyone who cheered me on while catching all my dangling modifiers and missing antecedents: Elizabeth Maddrey, Shari Schroeder, and Kay Springsteen. You're each invaluable.

About the Author

Heather loves coffee, God, her family, and laughter – not necessarily in that order! She writes approachable characters who, through the highs and lows of life, find a way to love God, embrace each day, and laugh out loud right along with her. And, yeah, her books almost always have someone who's a coffee addict. Some things just can't be helped.

She takes joy in creating characters that, much like her, are *flawed...but loved anyway.*

You can find Heather online at
http://www.heathergraywriting.com.

Other Books by Heather Gray

Informal Romance
An Informal Christmas
An Informal Arrangement
An Informal Introduction
An Informal Date
An Informal Affair
An Informal Reception (coming fall 2018)

Rainbow Falls (contemporary Christian romance)
Skye (coming January 2018)
Sunny (coming summer 2018)

Ladies of Larkspur (Inspirational Western Romance)
Mail Order Man
Just Dessert
Redemption

Regency Refuge (Inspirational Regency Romance)
His Saving Grace
Jackal
Queen

Contemporary Stand-Alone Inspirational Romance
Ten Million Reasons
Nowhere for Christmas

PREVIEW

An Informal Christmas
Informal Romance Book 1

If you liked *An Informal Affair*, then you'll enjoy the 2016 Selah Award winning novella *An Informal Christmas*.

Chapter One

Rylie ran for the elevator. A man in a faded denim jacket stood inside with the back curve of his left shoulder facing her. He didn't acknowledge her high-speed sprint in his direction. Nor did he stop the two brushed steel panels from sliding closed between them.

She thought of pushing the button and forcing the doors to reopen. Honestly, though, did she want to get stuck in a metal box with a man who didn't care about basic courtesy toward his fellow mankind? Not likely. Rylie huffed out an exasperated breath as she started up the stairs. Three flights up. It could be worse.

With a shove to the door, she exited the stairwell and stood on a narrow landing with skylights above and a view of the hospital's lobby below. Ten steps to the left, and she broke through to the hallway-of-no-return. Nobody came up to this floor unless they worked in one of the three departments exiled here. The first door belonged to the chaplaincy. The second led to the main office for the hospital social workers. The third door, decorated with construction paper butterflies and cotton ball caterpillars, was home sweet home — Child Life.

"I can't believe how rude people have become!" Rylie vented about the man in the elevator as she stepped past the colorful decorations and into her domain. Suzie, the part-time department head who kept their ship running tighter than junior size spandex on a burly linebacker, wasn't at her desk. Their offices were anything but spacious, though, so she was likely still within hearing distance. After all, what was a good venting without someone to listen?

"I was running for the elevator, but the guy inside didn't even wait for me. He let the doors slide closed. Because obviously it wasn't big enough for two of us." She left out the part about his back being to her. Absolving him of guilt wasn't high on her priority list at the moment.

Suzie emerged from The Vault, a nether region of their office used for storage. She dusted her hands off and frowned at Rylie. "We have company." She waved at the man following behind her. "This is Mr. York. He brought several boxes of stuffed animals for our kids."

No way. Not... Lots of guys wore denim jackets, right? It couldn't be the same...

"Sorry about the elevator. I got wedged into position by my dolly. I thought I heard someone calling, but by the time I turned myself around, the doors were closed and I was on my way up here." His voice reminded her of a lemon tart, decadent smoothness with a sharp aftertaste. For some reason, she found herself tempted to savor the sound rather than pucker. Too bad her mind was already made up about him. He might have proven interesting.

Guilt gnawed at her middle. *Sorry, God. I'll be nicer once I catch up on my sleep.* She sighed. *Okay, now I'm making excuses.*

"Yeah, well, no worries." Rylie waved a hand dismissively and slipped past him to reach her desk.

Had there been a dolly in the elevator with him? She didn't remember seeing one, but her single-minded irritation at the world might have prevented her from noticing it. She couldn't worry about that now, though. One of her kids was scheduled to start chemo later in the day. Two were going down for CT scans. Yet another had bone cancer that had led to discussion of amputation. The potential amputee didn't seem to mind — he was still at the age where scars were to be boasted about and *prosthesis* meant something super-cool and possibly cybernetic. His parents, on the other hand, were pushing the outer edge of hysteria.

And then there was Makayla.

In and out of the hospital most of her life, she was sixteen and full of spirit. Confinement to the pediatric oncology unit didn't suit her in the least. Makayla never meant to make trouble, but she always somehow managed to end up smack dab in the middle of it. This time she'd started a petition for Fourth of July manicures. Now every girl in the unit wanted one. In red, white, and blue. The fourth was in three days. How was Rylie supposed to find time to search for patriotic nail polish on such short notice?

She ran her fingers through her stick-straight black hair and sighed. It would have to come out of her own pocket, too. Suzie had reminded her just last week. The Child Life budget was maxed out. They were dependent on donations at this point, and nobody had anticipated the whims of a sixteen-year-old girl well enough to donate red, white, and blue polish.

"Uh, Rylie, did you hear me?"

She looked up from her desk. Suzie stood there, her wide green eyes expectant.

"Sorry, Suz. My girls all want their nails decorated with the stars and stripes, and I need to figure out how to make it happen. What did you say?"

Suzie shook her head. "Polish isn't in the budget."

"I'll work something out."

The hulking form of Mr. York remained over Suzie's right shoulder. Not that he hulked exactly. His was the wiry build of an Olympic swimmer, and if forced to guess, Rylie would put him at a hair shy of six feet tall.

Suzie waved a hand in their guest's general direction. "Mr. York here is planning on making monthly deliveries to us. He'd like to be able to coordinate with someone so he's better informed about the needs of our patients. I hoped you could be his liaison. You know, keep him up to date, that sort of thing."

"Liaison? Isn't that your job?" Rylie regretted the words as soon as they passed her lips.

The middle-aged woman shook her head as a shadow dimmed her eyes. "I'm part-time since the cut backs, remember? My job is to keep this department running, but there isn't enough time in the schedule for me to handle everything that needs attention. If I don't start delegating, I'm going to lose my mind."

Suzie wasn't to blame. The hospital, not her, had decided Child Life needed only a part-time administrator. To run the entire department.

Rylie sighed.

Working at a children's hospital affiliated with a much larger adult hospital had tremendous benefits. Their patients had access to treatments and equipment that a smaller facility on its own wouldn't be able to provide. It had its share of drawbacks, too, though. One such drawback was money.

Decisions were made based on profit, and the adult hospital — with nearly four times as many beds — dominated the spreadsheet. As a result, the children's hospital found itself in an indefensible position whenever budget cuts were discussed. If the adult patients didn't demand a service, that service was deemed unnecessary.

Times were hard, and it was apparent nowhere more so than in this forgotten corner of the hospital where everybody worked themselves into exhaustion so the patients wouldn't feel the pinch of reduced budgets and staff.

"Very well. Give me a second, Mr. York." Rylie booted up her computer and sent a message out on the intranet that Child Life shared with Social Work and the Chaplaincy. *Need red, white, and blue nail polish for the girls in Oncology. Anybody have some?*

She counted to thirty, hoping for a return message. None came, so she shifted her attention to the man who now leaned against the wall opposite her cubicle, arms crossed. As she did so, she prepared to send her computer into hibernation. The mouse hovered over the *power down* icon as a beep reached her ears. Her fingers flew across the keyboard as she typed in the command to bring the intranet chat box to the front on her desktop.

Dollar store by my house had huge display earlier in week. I'll check on my way home this afternoon. How many bottles?

Bless her. Blossom, the retired CEO of a successful technology firm, had realized too late that she couldn't stand retirement. She now volunteered as a chaplain to fill her time. Per her choice, she worked with adults in her official duties, but off-the-unpaid-volunteer-clock she did whatever she could to help the children's hospital.

Two of each ought to do it. THANK YOU.

She hoped those girls realized they wouldn't be getting flags and fireworks on their nails. Her skills were limited. It would be a good day if she remembered to paint one nail red, the one after that white, and the next one blue. If they were smart, the girls would give each other manicures and leave her, at best artistically challenged, out of the fun altogether.

"Ah-hem." The man still leaning against the wall cleared his throat.

A quick glance at the clock told Rylie she needed to be on her way. The first of the CT scans was scheduled to start in fifteen minutes. Scotty, an eight-year-old patient, had asked her to accompany him because his parents were at work, and he didn't want to be alone.

"Walk with me, Mr. York." She brushed past him hoping her voice hadn't sounded as cold to his ears as it had to hers. It wasn't his fault she'd been running nonstop since coming through the hospital doors hours prior — or that the day's race was far from over.

A second later, the yell came from behind her. "Watch out!"

Rylie spun around in time to see a previously stacked column of boxes tumbling in her direction. Of course. The boxes with the marbles in them. Who had piled those blasted boxes so high? No one in touch with their sanity would be foolish enough to... Oh yeah. She'd done it. Because they'd needed the room.

A speedy jump saved her from most of the trauma, but the edge of one box landed on her left foot. Her yell filled their small office. Meanwhile, one of the other boxes broke open. Marbles began rolling across the floor. Rylie, her lost balance tossing her in that direction anyway, managed to throw herself in front of the door as she fell. At least the glass-orbs-of-doom wouldn't wander out into the hallway and cause further catastrophe.

Whose brilliant idea was it to donate a hundred pounds of marbles to the Child Life department? Now she remembered. The international marble champion Rylie had convinced to visit the hospital and host a demonstration for the children one afternoon had been so moved by the experience that he'd donated thousands of choking hazards to them. The boxes had been stacked in the corner so long she'd almost forgotten about them. Until now.

"It's awfully narrow in here. I brushed against a box. Sorry." Mr. York held his hand out to help her up, but Rylie wasn't sure she wanted to move. Some falls – and crushed toes – deserved to be babied for a bit. The image of poor Scotty, afraid of the CT machine, popped into her head, though, and she couldn't ignore the outstretched hand.

The benevolent stranger and knocker-over-of-boxes started to speak again, but Rylie cut him off as she got to her feet. "I'm needed elsewhere. Walk with me, or it'll have to wait."

"Don't worry about the mess here, folks. I have nothing better to do with my time." Suzie's indignant muttering followed them all the way to the elevator.

"You should get your foot examined."

Being angry at him would be easier if his voice didn't make her think of sweet treats on hot summer days.

"A little boy is going for an NBD test, but he's terrified. My job is to make it bearable for him, even if that means limping all the way there and back."

"NBD?"

"No Big Deal. The kids classify any procedure not involving needles, saws, or drills as NBD." The children actually said needles or a scalpel. She'd thrown *saws* and *drills* into the equation to get under his skin. Looks like it worked. So why didn't she feel good about it?

"Oh."

Rylie took a deep breath as the elevator eased down another floor. The time had come to start acting her age. Or even half her age. She wasn't exactly getting off to a good start with this man.

She held out her hand. "I'm Rylie Durham, the Child Life Specialist assigned to the oncology unit."

His hand enveloped hers in a warm grasp. "Zach York. I'm… the guy who knocks over boxes, gets himself jammed into elevators, and…" He rolled his eyes. "And apparently forgets his dolly up in the Child Life office so he has to go back for it later."

It was a trial, but she afforded him a smile. "What brings you to us?"

His shrug was a study in nonchalance. "Another time, maybe." He pulled something from his wallet and held it out to her. "Here's my card. Drop me an email within the next day or two so I know how to get in touch with you. When I'm ready to order some items for next month, I'll contact you and find out what y'all need."

She took the card but doubted any communication between them would be as simple as he made it sound. This man had complication written all over him.

"Ignore my email at your own risk, Ms. Durham." His molasses eyes glinted with a hint of mischievousness. "Or you might find yourself with more marbles instead of whatever children in the hospital actually need."

The elevator *dinged*, and the doors opened smoothly near the entrance to Oncology. Rylie stepped out but couldn't stop herself from glancing back at him. "Are you coming?"

"Not today. I need to fetch my dolly." He pushed the button that would return him to the forgotten corner of the hospital, and the doors slid closed.

Hm. He wanted to help the kids, but he wasn't eager to see them. He was either uptight, emotionally detached, or she was reading too much into his actions.

Tempted as she was, she couldn't take time to psychoanalyze the handsome Zach York. A wheelchair rolled her way, accompanied by a nurse. "Scotty! Sorry I'm late. You won't believe this, but a tower of marbles fell on me."

The little boy giggled and pointed to the foot she was favoring. "Is that where it landed?"

"Of course it is. You know I'm the clumsiest person in the whole world, right?"